A WILD COW WINTER

Wild Cow Ranch 2

Natalie Bright
Denise F. McAllister

A Wild Cow Winter
Natalie Bright
Denise F. McAllister

Paperback Edition

CKN Christian Publishing
An Imprint of Wolfpack Publishing
5130 S. Fort Apache Rd. 215-380
Las Vegas, NV 89148

Copyright © 2021

Paperback ISBN: 978-1-64734-265-4
Ebook ISBN: 978-1-64734-264-7

A WILD COW WINTER

Chapter One

Her hand trembled and the small print legalese on the page blurred. For a minute, Carli Jameson thought about all she'd been through to build this business. One swish of an ink pen would change her life forever.

"Miss Jameson, is there a problem?"

She looked up, pen poised over the signature line. The shiny, sleek boardroom table stretched out before her. A handsome, smiling attorney sat directly across watching her with a questioning gaze. Why couldn't she just sign the darn contract?

There were new adventures waiting for her. A new life. Perhaps a new love. And yet just being back in Georgia and stepping into her old life promised comfort and safety. The problems in Texas seemed like a million miles away.

With a flourish of bright purple from her hair to her shoes, Adelphia Fenwick, attorney-at-law, entered the conference room in downtown Atlanta, her briefcase landing with a thunk on the table. "Sorry I'm late, Carli. Crazy traffic."

She offered a hand across the table. "Jim. Good to see you again."

While the attorneys talked, their voices sounded like white noise in Carli's head. The names of her riding students and their horses lingered in her mind. She smiled remembering each one's funny issues and quirks. She was leaving the equine business in good hands. Bringing in a partner had been one of the best moves she had ever made, even though that partner hated her now. His offer being more than fair, it was enough capital to keep the ranch she had inherited in the black until cattle prices improved. And pay taxes, or more specifically inheritance tax. Another worry that niggled her thoughts late at night.

"Carli, do you have any questions?" Del plopped into the leather chair beside her and rolled it closer. Under her breath the lawyer added, "It's all in order, just like we discussed. Is everything all right?"

"Yes. Fine." Carli cleared her throat. Change was not an easy thing for her. With her heart jumping inside her chest, anxiety stole her confidence, and yet over the past few weeks she felt joy like she'd never known before. But walking away from everything she had built here was hard.

The easy way would be to slide back into her old life. The routine was so familiar. The most difficult choice was to face the challenges of a move halfway across the country to embrace a life she knew nothing about. But then life had never granted her the easy road.

With precise penmanship, and a certain amount of resignation to change, she signed her name, Carlotta Jean Jameson. The Saddlebag Equine Center was no longer hers.

"Sorry I'm late." The familiar voice made her gasp softly. Mark Copeland, her soon-to-be ex-business partner. "Has she signed?"

He never looked in her direction, only spoke directly to the other attorney.

"Yes, I signed." She willed him to look at her. It hurt that he had been her best friend for so long, and now he couldn't even acknowledge she was in the same room.

The attorney pulled the contract across the table and Mark sat, picked up a pen, and signed his name before looking at her. "I suppose you'll be out to get your stuff?"

"Sure. I'll see you soon." She stood, they shook hands all around, except Mark didn't offer his hand to her. Carli followed Del to the elevators as she tried to tame the myriad of emotions that swirled through her. She hated to leave burned bridges behind.

"How are you liking Texas so far?" Del asked.

"It's so different," said Carli. "I miss the streams and woods of Georgia, but I'm beginning to appreciate the wide and treeless grassy plains. The sunrises and sunsets are so unique and amazing. I hate missing a single one." She hesitated. "Thanks for working on this, Del."

"Change isn't easy. And giving up on the business you worked so hard to create is difficult too. But you can't turn down that inheritance. It's not every day you get a 22,000-acre spread complete with cows, a beautiful headquarters, and Texas cowboys. Step into your new life, Carli, and don't look back."

Good advice. She didn't have a choice now. And by the time the elevator reached the ground floor, her step did seem a bit lighter. She could run a ranch. Why not? She could learn, plus she had a great group of people more than willing to teach her and help. She felt ready to take on any new challenges that God sent her way. One thing was for certain—she'd grown in her faith recently. She had to believe in that faith and know that she was on the right path.

Del gave her a quick hug and last-minute instructions on how the transfer of funds would take place. They waved goodbye. As Carli walked to the back lot where she had parked her pickup truck and livestock trailer, she thought about talking to Mark again. He had been more than a business partner. A riding coach, best friend, and the one person she completely trusted to always have her back. She loved him like a brother, but he wanted more. And that was the problem.

Before she drove out to the house to pack up the rest of her things, there was one more place she wanted to see.

The Georgia International Horse Park was bursting with pickup trucks and livestock trailers of every color. Riders in brightly colored shirts eased their horses through the lot, while some milled about near the barn entrances. Carli loved this place. She had spent many hours here, both as a competitor and riding instructor. The hustle and bustle made her yearn for her horse Beau. They had certainly been a team to watch, and she had loved every minute of competition.

As she walked through the stalls area, she stopped to take in the sights and smell the familiar scent of hay and dust, sweat and manure. She would always have many fond memories of this place. She paused and surveyed the scene, seeing a few familiar faces.

For whatever reason, she wanted, needed, to see her old stomping grounds before heading back to Texas. It seemed true though—you can't go home. It's never the same. She felt like she was seeing ghosts, an image of herself when she used to show here all the time.

A bubbly voice caused a sudden sour taste in her mouth. Savannah. The one girl who had dogged her, not only in competition but in love as well. Carli clenched her fists and said a silent prayer that her old boyfriend wasn't there too. She tried to duck and go in the opposite direction, but a swirl of rhinestones and long hair couldn't be ignored particularly when it was calling your name.

"Carli! Yoo hoo! Carli!"

She turned slowly and faced her nemesis. "Savannah. How are you?"

"Is it true you inherited a cow farm?"

"A ranch. Yes, I did."

"In Texas?" she giggled. "I can't imagine you and Beau riding across the prairie chasing cows."

"Well, that's me."

"About that whole drugging thing and our last competition ending so awful for you, I'm just glad you're back on your feet."

"Thanks. I'm trying to move forward."

A good-looking cowboy slid up next to Savannah and gave her a peck on her neck. She giggled again. "This is Marco. He's a bull rider."

Carli smiled and the handsome cowboy returned her glance with a wink. He wasn't her Josh, the Josh that Savannah had stolen. This was certainly worth her stopping by the horse park. Knowing that Josh didn't still have Savannah, or Carli. She wished him a good life, wherever he might be. And surprisingly, her first thought was not a desire to run back to him, even though she had previously thought he was "the one". Now it was a Wild Cow Ranch cowpuncher's face that she thought of instead.

"I've got to get on out to my house and pack the rest of my things." Carli turned on her heels and walked away.

"If I'm ever in Texas, I'll look you up," Savannah called at her back.

Carli raised one arm in a wave but didn't turn around. She made a beeline to the parking lot and her truck. One thing she knew for certain. This wasn't her home any longer. She belonged in Texas.

She truly believed God had set her on this path. She didn't know why or how, but she had to follow it.

Chapter Two

A done deal. Carli signed away her interest in the equine business she had partnered with Mark Copeland for the last eight years or so. She felt a weight had been lifted off her shoulders, and yet she felt sad over the strain this put on their ability to even look at each other.

They'd been through thick and thin, and she always valued his friendship. But turned out he wanted more from her—romance—which had caught her totally off guard, and she just couldn't give him that. Mark was her best friend. The first person she had run to for support and encouragement. A business partner she had dreamed and schemed with for almost a decade, and she would always love him like a brother. Of course, he was hurt and angered. She had turned her back on all that they had built and moved to a ranch she inherited from a grandfather she had never known.

What a strange day it had been already. The meeting this morning at a downtown Atlanta law office to sign the papers which made the Saddlebag

Equine Center officially now all Mark's.

Then her quick trip to the Georgia International Horse Park in Conyers where she knew a horse show would be taking place. All those memories of showing there, with Mark, loomed in her head. And with her boyfriend, Josh. But she didn't see Josh today. In fact, Mark had told her on his trip to Texas that Josh and Savannah had been planning marriage.

That obviously didn't happen. Carli had run into Savannah. With a new guy. A bull rider named Marco. Carli always had a feeling about Savannah, and it wasn't very nice. Savannah seemed to go through men like the flavor of the month ice cream.

Carli steered her truck and trailer onto the gravel driveway of Saddlebag Lane where her little bungalow house was, and where she and Mark had boarded a few riding clients' horses. But things looked different now. Maybe you really couldn't go home. Nothing stays the same.

The beep of a bulldozer's engine as it backed up caught her attention. On the far side of the yard, the machinery knocked down a row of trees where the round pen for lunging horses had stood when Carli lived there. She parked her truck and trailer next to a row of other trucks.

Mark stood with a group of men watching the bulldozer work. When he saw Carli get out of her vehicle, he came towards her.

"I put your stuff in that storage shed out back."

No hug hello, how're you doing. No small talk about the changes that were taking place right in front of their eyes. It was good seeing him again, but this conversation wasn't going to be easy.

She'd have to initiate the conversation. "Are you putting in an arena? What did the landlord say about that?"

Mark gave her a stony face. "I bought the place. Yes, I'm building an arena."

It was tough getting information out of him, but she wanted to know. "Are you living in the house?"

"No, I'm going to tear it down. Build a bigger one."

That comment pierced her heart some. That was her tiny house. It had been her little refuge where she scrimped and saved while working at the real estate office, but desperately wanting to work with horses fulltime. She remembered taping magazine pages that depicted Western artwork to her plain walls, never being able to afford pictures or decorations of any kind.

Now Mark was going to demolish her memories. But she knew she couldn't hold it against him. She couldn't be in two places at once—Georgia and Texas. She had made her decision.

"Wow, Mark, business must be really good. How many riding clients do you have? What about the barn? Will it be big enough for all the horses?"

"No. That's getting torn down also. And, yes, business is good. But this place isn't your concern any longer."

He didn't really look at her but kept his eye on the bulldozer and the other men.

"Carli, I'm kind of in the middle of a meeting with my partners. The storage shed is unlocked. Do you need anything else?"

That hit her in the gut. He obviously didn't want to be friends. No offer to help move any of her things into the trailer. No "let bygones be bygones". She really shouldn't be surprised. That's how her life had gone for as long as she could remember. People came into it and people left, sometimes abruptly. She wouldn't let Mark hurt her any more than he had. And she realized he was nursing his own heartache. Plus, she reminded herself to do what God would want her to do, to try to be civil and understanding. It was hard, but she did not want to be vindictive or mean.

"No, I don't need anything. I can manage on my own. I've been doing it all my life."

He started to walk away, but she stopped him. "Mark, I just want to say I'm happy for you. I'm sorry we couldn't stay friends, but I really wish you all the best for a good future and a happy life. If you ever need anything, don't hesitate to contact me."

He nodded slightly and mumbled, "Goodbye, Carli."

Turning her back on Mark, she made her way through the vehicles and workers to the back of the barn. She opened the storage shed and pulled some things out to get a better look at them. It was too hot to be inside. A trickle of sweat slid down the middle of her back.

There was a rickety rattan couch, a bean bag chair, and a small, round table with four chairs. All from Goodwill. An old mattress she had had forever, also second hand. Looking through some of the boxes, she found a set of chipped dishware, mismatched glasses, and an eclectic collection of coffee mugs from various horse shows.

One box revealed some paperwork, tax returns, old bills, a few photos of her with her horses at competitions. She dropped to her knees and shuffled through the contents, stopping to look at the pictures. In one, she sat tall and proud in the saddle, with Mark standing next to her either holding the reins or with a hand on the horse's neck. In one photo, he leaned close with his hand resting on her thigh. Bright smiles covered both their faces.

That box she tucked under one arm and placed it in the backseat of her pickup truck. She walked back to the shed and paused for a minute to stare at the contents, suddenly realizing she did not want any of it. This had been who she was before, but she was nothing like that person now. She closed the door and walked away.

As she made her way back to the truck, she thought about all the things she wanted to tell Mark. There was so much left unsaid between them.

Life was a strange thing. Sometimes one person's perception of a situation was completely different from another's. They might conjure up a whole fantasy of how they think things should be. That's what Mark had done, unbeknownst to Carli. Did he have those feelings for her all those years? Now she felt like a fool. She never meant to lead him on, and from her viewpoint she hadn't. They were just friends. Horse showing, running their business together. She was blindsided when he had recently shown up in Texas at the ranch she had inherited and confessed his feelings for her. He even kissed her which was a shock. He had never conveyed romance to her before or even flirted with her in any way. Mark had always been work, work, work.

She dug through the box of photos again and

walked over to Mark who was surrounded by the other men all engaged in laughter. He frowned when she approached.

"Mark, sorry to interrupt." She reached towards him with a photo in hand. "And here's a memory for you, if you want. It's you and me at the Big A show. Thanks for everything. Take care."

He just stared at her, not in a mean way, but with an emotionless expression of indifference. He didn't seem to care what she did.

With that, she turned to go. Carli needed to get back to her home in Texas. And the people who were waiting for her. At the Wild Cow Ranch.

She unhooked the old livestock trailer from behind her truck, gave it a quick pat as she thought about the countless miles she'd logged pulling her horse Beau to shows and competitions, and then drove away. She never looked in the rearview mirror.

Chapter Three

"Now, Buck, I thought everything was decided." Lola Wallace gave her husband a hard look. "We told Rena we'd be there. You can't all of a sudden change your mind. Other people are involved." Lola was more than a little perturbed with him.

Warming up leftovers on a plate for his dinner, she didn't make anything for herself. Too nervous, too upset. Typical of her being a tiny bundle of energy, she hovered over the table since this was important. She needed an answer. Getting her husband to set aside his foreman duties and take a few days away from the Wild Cow Ranch was next to impossible, but his sense of duty was one of the things she loved about him.

"Buck, we talked about this. Carli is on her way back from Georgia and she can handle the ranch work for a few days. I thought you said you can go over everything with her—how to break ice in the troughs if it gets really cold, feeding the cows the cake pellets, how to light the pilot on the stove."

"I think she'll do all right," he said quietly. "But

Lank is going to be gone too."

"So, what's the problem? Don't you think she can handle things while we're gone?"

"That's just it, Lola. I don't know. She'll be all alone on the ranch. Wonder if something goes wrong?"

"And Lank will be in Amarillo at his sister's, right? That's less than an hour away. If she needs anything, she can call him. He can be out here in no time and check on Carli." Lola filled up his iced tea glass and sat down beside him.

"Yeah, he could. But he's supposed to be visiting with his sister and her family, those little nephews of his. This being the first Christmas without his mother. He needs to get away from here."

"I know, Buck. And so do you. But our trip has been planned for a while now. We promised Rena. What do you expect me to tell our niece? She's been looking forward to our visit and I'm sure she has things planned. Do you want to ruin her Christmas? Do you want me to tell Rena that we can't come now?"

Buck frowned and looked at his wife. "No, Lola. I don't suppose we can do that."

They had helped their niece Rena in the past. And they worried about her at times. She was a hard-working, sweet, young woman who had had her share of trials—mostly due to bad roommate situations or disappointing job positions.

There was the time when Rena was first out on her own and shared a house with three other girls. One ended up bringing boys home to stay over-night, another was found to be stealing from all the girls, and the third one disappeared in the night without paying her share of the rent.

Rena's mother tried to help as best she could, but she was a widow on a tight budget. So, it was Buck and Lola to the rescue.

Another roommate experience involved one girl who had a penchant for loud music at all hours. She also liked to cook liver and onions in the middle of the night, which interrupted Rena's sleep that she needed for her job the next day. Not to mention the girl nearly burned the house down with her botched cooking attempts or when she forgot to blow out candles in her bedroom.

And speaking of Rena's jobs, one boss had money troubles and couldn't give Rena a paycheck for three weeks. Then the check bounced when she did get it. Again, Buck and Lola helped her out during a tough time. That employer ended up in some sort of scandal that was publicized in the newspaper and Rena had no choice but to quit and look for another job.

Rena's troubles weighed heavy on Lola's mind, and she wanted their niece to know they'd always be there for her.

"Buck, what are you thinking?"

He was silent for what seemed like a very long time, his brows drawn together in an agonized expression.

Then he tilted his head and looked at his wife. "I would never want to hurt Rena. She's like a daughter to us."

"Yes, she is." Lola nodded in agreement.

He rubbed his hands back and forth. "You're gonna think this is crazy but I'm starting to think of Carli that way. I know she's only been here a short time. Maybe it's because we knew her grand-parents."

"I know." Lola laid a hand on his shoulder. "I'm beginning to feel the same way about her. It's her whole story that tears at my heart. A mother that abandoned her. Grandparents that searched for her but died before she was found and returned to the Wild Cow. And after the barn fire, how she came to know the Lord. She's a babe when it comes to her faith. She's still learning what it all means for her life. I guess I feel real protective of Carli like I do of Rena. I know you do too."

His face went grim. "I think of what-ifs. What if the feeder truck breaks down? Carli won't know how to fix it. What if the horses or cows get sick or hurt? God forbid, what if Carli gets sick or hurt? Is she ready for the responsibility?"

Rarely did worry get the better of this man who accepted hard times with a calm reserve and un-wavering faith that Lola had always admired. She would have to be the strong one now. She was going to put her foot down on this one.

That's how their marriage had stood the test of time. Through any kind of struggle, one was strong when the other was weak. And most importantly, they never let go of their faith. When it seemed like one of them did, or was struggling, the other picked it up to remind them that they would be lost without it.

"Buck, my sweet husband." She took his face in both her hands and locked eyes. "You have a heart of gold and I love you for that. I know that you love both girls—Rena, our flesh and blood, and now this new young woman, Carli, whose life is tied to the

Wild Cow Ranch. You want to help both of them. And you can, Buck. I also think God wants us to have husband and wife alone time. He doesn't want us to run ourselves ragged because we'll be no good to anyone else. He wants us to protect our health, physical and mental, so we can continue doing good things in His name. And one of the biggest things we've learned, husband of mine..."

Buck smiled and they looked lovingly at each other.

Lola continued, "...one of the biggest things we've learned during our faith walk together is trust. Trust each other. Trust God. Even when we don't feel like it. Even when we want to take matters into our own hands and control everything around us. I feel we should stick with our plans. We need to go see Rena. I think Carli will do just fine here alone and it will build her confidence. Let her discover what she's made of. You're always telling me to trust Him. Things will work out. John 14:1 says, 'Let not your hearts be troubled.' Jeremiah 17:7 says, 'Blessed is the man who trusts in the Lord.'"

"You just want to go shopping in Dallas," Buck said. Amusement flickered in his eyes.

"That's true," Lola laughed and gave him a kiss on the cheek. "What do you say, dear husband? Can we do that? Can we trust God? Take a deep breath and put everything in His capable hands. Then we can relax and go on our trip, with peace of mind, the peace He gives us."

Buck nodded in agreement and held up his hands. "Okay, you win. How did you get so smart, beautiful wife of mine?" He gave her an irresistible grin. The one that still made her knees go weak.

"I think it's from hanging out with you." She laughed.

They gave each other such a sweet kiss that swept all their worries away.

At least for tonight.

Chapter Four

The Wild Cow Ranch, Texas Panhandle

Carli Jameson stood in the alley of the corral with one arm resting on the top gate rail. Her breath hung in the air as she stomped her feet to stay warm. The sun had only been up a couple of hours, and, typical for December, it had yet to take the chill from the air. Other cowboys stood at various spots along the pen alley, each with a specific job to do. A dust cloud hung over them created by trampling hooves. The bawling of the cows and the answered calls from their calves drowned out the ability to talk. Today was shipping day.

Her job was to open the gate for the heifers as they were sorted from the herd. The crew worked with practiced precision. A cowboy on horseback cut about ten calves from the main group and ran them up the alley where several men on foot sorted by heifer or steer. The first group pushed them to the next crew of cowboys who directed them into another alley using long poles with flags on the ends. Their shouts rang out.

"Heifer."

"Heifer."

That was Carli's cue to be ready. She swung the gate, and the excited calves ran towards the opening, except one turned at the last minute in a panic and tried to go around her. She stepped out from behind the gate and raised her arms, "Yaah!"

The calf spun and shot through the opening.

Dayworking cowboys made it look easy, just like a well-oiled machine, except Carli felt like a broken cog in the wheel. She tried to pay attention and anticipate what came next. The hardest thing about cow work was knowing how to stay out of the way.

These hands worked together many times over the course of a year on various ranches, and instinctively knew what to do without speaking a word. She was trying to learn and absorb everything she could about cattle ranching.

The Wild Cow Ranch belonged to her now. She inherited it from her mother's father, Grandpa Ward, who changed his Last Will and then died a short month later. Carli never knew him, or any of her mother's family. Although, she vaguely remembered meeting him once when she was about ten. Her mother, Michelle, at sixteen years old, gave her baby to a sweet older couple to foster. Carli was born in Amarillo, Texas, then grew up in Florida and Georgia. She had a good life with the Fitzgeralds, but a piece of her always felt off kilter. Out of place. And now Carli owned the very Texas ranch that her mother had been determined to run away from.

"Looks like you're getting the hang of it," said Lank Torres, the ranch's cowhand. Her employee. His neatly shaped black mustache and chin patch encircled the wide grin that reached his sparkling blue-gray eyes. Those eyes always made her utterly weak at the knees. It was disgusting. She hated feeling out of control around him.

"Thanks for the pointers. I'm not as quick as the others." She glanced over the backs of the herd at her neighbor, Nathan Olsen, who gave her a thumbs up. She grinned back at him. He sat on his horse in the next pen wearing a bright purple pearl snap shirt, a black wild rag around his neck, and a black cowboy hat. Handsome and all Texan, he looked like he had just stepped out of a Western wear catalog. Why couldn't he make her pulse race? Dating a neighbor just seemed more appropriate than dating one of her employees.

"You'll get the hang of it, boss." Lank looked towards the ranch's entrance. "The bull haulers are here."

Carli turned her attention away from Lank to watch a line of 18-wheelers rumble into ranch headquarters. The culmination of a year's work ended with shipping day. The heifers were going to a ranch in Kansas to become mommas and help to build someone else's cow/calf operation. The steers were going to a feeder in Nebraska. One of the trucks had a small green wreath wired to the grill. She cringed. Out in the middle of nowhere and still there's a reminder of the holiday she tries to avoid at all costs.

Carli glanced at her bottle-fed calf, Maverick, in a nearby pen. She had absolutely refused to allow

Lank and Buck Wallace, her ranch foreman, to make him into a steer. Little Maverick had been orphaned, born well after the other calves in the herd; his momma was sick and injured before being set upon by a pack of coyotes. Maverick was hiding, curled up in a clump of yucca near his dead mother. Staying put right where his momma told him to be. But he was gaunt and starved so he took to the bottle without much trouble. He was Carli's and she was his. She loved him almost as much as she loved her horse Beau. Who knew back in Georgia that she'd end up having emotional ties to a cow?

Maverick bawled in answer to the other cries and moans, peering out from between two slats. Lank and Carli shut him in a small stall to keep him out of the way.

"Steer."

"Steer."

"Steer."

The declarations rang out as three calves bounded around the corner. Carli heard the man's shout above the bawling and stepped inside the pen with the heifers, hiding behind her gate. Three steers sporting orange ear tags ran past her without any trouble and then through an opening into another pen. A third pen held calves with white ear tags. They were over half done with the sorting.

"What are those calves?" Carli asked Buck while he waited for the cowboys on horseback to cut out the next group to be sorted.

"Replacements. Heifers we're keeping. They'll be put with low birthweight bulls and become calf producers for the Wild Cow. They get to stay home."

Carli didn't know much about Red Angus, but she was learning. Solid colored in varying shades of rusty red. Soft eyes with long eyelashes set in delicate faces watched her cautiously. "They're pretty."

"I pick out the ones with more feminine faces. They make good mothers," Buck said.

The continuous beep of an 18-wheeler backing up to the loading chute rose above the bawling calls of the mommas and their babies. The early morning sun cast a brilliant reflection on the shiny metal rig. A second too late she heard, "Heifer!" Her gate was only part way open and the men behind the calf came around the corner flapping their flags and making "whoop" sounds.

Four hundred pounds of beefsteak plowed right over her. The calf's shoulder bumped her side and Carli spun and toppled to the dirt. Lank sprang into action and swung the gate shut before the entire lot of heifers escaped. The runaway heifer reached a dead end in the alley, twisted and turned, and decided she needed another piece of Carli. But she was ready this time. She jumped to the fence a split second quick enough to get out of the way but lost her balance and the momentum sent her toppling into the pen on the other side. She landed with a hard thud. Lank swung the gate open and the heifer came charging into the pen. Nathan appeared at her side and blocked the heifer from running over her again. He offered her a hand up and Carli let him slowly pull her to her feet.

"Is anything broken?" Nathan asked.

"Good job using your body as a blocking dummy." Lank smirked as he gave her a sideways grin.

Carli brushed the dust from the back of her jeans. That was going to be sore tomorrow. "Just trying to make a hand." Everyone laughed.

The dayworking crew finished sorting the herd. Buck motioned for Carli to follow him. "You can record the information in our ranch book as we get a weight."

They stood at the scales, a sizable contraption with a numbered bar housed inside a tin shed. The floor floated inside a cage, with pipe rail fencing all around and openings at both ends. Cowboys ran fifteen head into the pen and closed the gate which clanked shut. Buck moved the weights on the bar. He called out the total which Carli wrote down in a notebook. As the calves were pushed out the other end, two cowboys took a second headcount. Buck showed Carli how to do the math to get an average weight. After all the herd was weighed, they were pushed down the alley and up the chute into the waiting livestock trailer.

The trucks backed up to the loading chute one by one. The cattle were urged up the ramp, their hooves clanking on the metal as they filled every space in the two-level trailer. The truck driver walked into the trailer behind each small group, directing calves into the belly, a handful to the very front, and others up a second ramp into the top level. Each section was separated by a gate which clanked shut in between.

The cowpunchers worked steadily, without much talk as they sorted, weighed, and loaded the year's calves. Carli watched the last truck driver slam the trailer gates shut, check them to make sure they latched, and then walk all around his rig, giving it a once-over. He climbed into the cab and drove up the hill. The last load.

A sadness swept over Carli as she watched the taillights of the bull hauler. Those calves were born and raised on the Wild Cow. They were a part of a decades-old legacy begun by her grandfather. Their life had been as good as it could have possibly been, and they were as much a part of the land as she was. The good thing was knowing that the heifers were leaving to form the basis of a herd for somebody else. The steers were product, in the same way as the farmers who raise watermelons or grass hay.

"That's good work, cowboys. We can take the replacement heifers back to their pasture." A ringing chow bell interrupted him. Buck grinned. "But let's eat first."

The group walked towards the cookhouse, spurs jingling and boots crunching the gravel drive. Carli followed behind trying not to limp, but her hip was screaming at her.

"How about I get you some aspirin for that?" murmured Nathan as he fell into step beside her.

She smiled up at him. "Thanks, but I'll survive."

Lank ran up on the other side of her. "Shake it off, cowboy. We have more work to do after lunch." He swatted her on the back and hurried past them into the cookhouse. Nathan stopped to hold the door for her.

She glared at Lank's back as he dashed inside. Carli stopped at the threshold, the swirling smells of cinnamon and chili peppers tickled her nose. She closed her eyes for a brief minute, taking a deep breath to savor the aroma, but hesitated. Slowly opening her eyes, Nathan gave her a funny look as he held the door open for her and waited.

Come on. You can do this. She forced herself to take a step inside the cookhouse and face the scene she knew was waiting. She frowned.

Christmas.

On every flat surface, wall, staircase banister. Everywhere.

The ranch cookhouse was a gluttonous display of the season. A needle-sharp headache hit Carli right behind the eyes as Here Comes Santa Claus pierced her ears. She took a deep breath and frowned at the towering tree that stood by the fireplace. A colossal reminder of how much she hated this time of year.

Chapter Five

The giant Christmas tree in the Wild Cow Ranch cookhouse was a gaudy display of holiday ornaments gone wild. What must have been a million twinkling fairy lights made Carli squint if she looked directly at them. Not one branch was spared. The ten-foot tree was smothered in red and white checkered bows. Small wreaths fashioned from barbed wire and decorated with tiny clumps of greenery along with glistening red satin balls. A train track encircled the tree trunk, providing the direction for a small locomotive that chugged around and around. Its coal cars were filled with chocolate M&M candies. The clickety-clack of its tiny wheels echoed in the dining hall, rising above the friendly banter of the dayworkers.

A stone fireplace rose to the twenty-foot ceiling; its mantel could not possibly hold any more garland. In fact, Carli wondered at how the heap stayed in place. The pine scent assaulted her senses as she stood next to it, waiting her turn to fill her plate. She sniffled and rubbed her nose.

Lola Wallace, Buck's wife, stepped out of the kitchen into the dining hall to punch the button on the CD player. The dayworkers bowed their heads as Buck led them in a prayer to thank God for a safe morning and to bless the food. Carli said a silent prayer that someone would forget to turn the music back on. Keep Lola busy please, Lord. Is it all right to pray for such things?

The spread laid out on the counter that separated the kitchen from the dining hall included Lola's specialty, beef enchiladas. Carli let the cowboys fill their plates first. They had worked hard that morning. While she waited at the end of the line, she turned her back to the gigantic tree, but then had to face the dining hall. It was a Christmas explosion, too, and no blank space had been spared. The sight made her stomach queasy.

More garlands hung from the stair banister and across the second-floor balcony railing, held in place by huge red satin bows. Carli wondered if the upstairs bedrooms and bathrooms were decorated as well. She couldn't even imagine what Lola and Buck's bedroom must look like.

Greenery hung over every window, adorned with red berry wreaths.

Instead of desserts, the sideboard served as the setting for a Christmas village, more elaborate than anything Carli had ever seen. Nestled in soft piles of cotton were various sizes and shapes of little shops and houses. The tiny windows sparkled with golden light. Each building was surrounded by snow-covered evergreens, miniature people, and horse-drawn sleds. An ornate white chapel dominated center stage, its steeple rising high above the quaint village.

Lola had really outdone herself, both on the food and the decorations.

The couple who raised Carli weren't much on holidays or celebration. With just the three of them, there was only a small table-top tree, a few presents for Carli, ham and pumpkin pie, then Christmas was over in a flash. Carli never knew any of her blood relatives and her guardians never spoke of them. After the Fitzgeralds died, both in the same year, she spent Christmas Day by herself. Alone. It was just another day. She hated the commercialization, the fuss over toys and gifts, and the decadence of gorging on food, all for one day of the year. It made no sense to her.

"Everything go smoothly this morning?" Lola asked Carli from the other side of the granite bar.

Carli lifted a holly berry-edged plate from the stack. She frowned at the red napkin with reindeer faces before shoving it and silverware into her back pocket. Trying to ignore the dinnerware, she dug into the dish of cheesy enchiladas and then covered the other half of her plate with refried beans and Spanish rice. She skipped the salad this time but got extra salsa. It seemed that becoming a Texan brought with it a new appreciation for hot sauce. Lola served it at every meal. Homemade, a special family recipe. She glanced at Lola. "Yes. Calves look good. I was sorta sad to see them go."

"I feel that way, too. They've lived their whole life here. They're part of our ranch family." Lola smiled.

"But we do our best to produce healthy beef and the money they bring keeps us going for another year, so I try not to think about it. Here, be sure and try my guacamole. You need some hot sauce, too."

Since moving to the ranch, Carli gave up on refusing the food that Lola shoved her way. She gained weight, but that only made her want to work harder. Turns out the added calories gave her more energy and made it easier to keep up with her ranch employees, Lank and Buck. She loved staying outside most days and working at all the chores that needed to be done. Her office job back in Georgia was a distant memory; she sure didn't miss it. And since she had her horse, Beau, with her too, there wasn't much that she longed for from her old home. Horse shows and giving riding lessons had been traded for a cattle operation. Ranch work was very satisfying. She just needed to learn more about the business.

Carli took the empty seat next to Lank. She noticed he absentmindedly pushed food around on his plate, eyes staring out one of the windows. Sadness clouded his face.

"Does Lola decorate like this every year?"

"Yep," Lank mumbled.

"What are you pouting about?" Carli asked, even though she didn't expect a detailed answer. They had a good working relationship, even shared a kiss. A giant mistake on her part and one that would never be repeated. She resisted the urge to place her hand on his arm. She basically resisted all her feelings for him on a daily basis. As the ranch owner and his employer, it wouldn't be proper for her to ignite something between them.

Nathan sat down on her other side. "Why all the gloomy faces?"

"I hate Christmas." She shoveled a bite of beans and rice into her mouth. "And Lank appears to be in a mood. I thought the morning went great, so I don't know what's going on with him."

Lank snapped his head around and looked at her. "This used to be my favorite time of year. Reminds me of my mom."

"Your mother passed away first of the year? Sorry, man." Nathan stopped eating to cast a sincere look of sympathy at him.

"This will be my family's first Christmas without her." Lank rose from the table, scraped the food off his plate into the trash, and left.

"He never skips dessert. And it's sopapilla cheesecake. He usually eats half of the dish on his own." She watched Lank leave, the front door slamming after him.

"His mother died of cancer, right after the holidays. I think he and his sister spent most of last Christmas and New Year's at the hospital. It must have been a horrible time for them. This holiday isn't going to be easy."

Carli stopped chewing as a flush of guilt washed over her. She had been insensitive to Lank's feelings. "That must have been terrible for Lank and his sister. As I was saying, I don't understand all the fuss. There's nothing special about Christmas for me."

"You haven't spent a Christmas at the Rafter O Ranch then."

"How is your family any different? Just another meal like any other day except with tacky green and red tinsel everywhere."

Nathan's mouth opened and he stared at her in shock. "Just another meal? You've got to be kidding me."

"I call it as I see it." Carli glanced at Nathan as he kept staring at her. Obviously, he wanted to say something but was holding back. "Out with it. Say what you got to say."

He took a sip of iced sweet tea, looked up at her again with those clear blue eyes. "This time of year means a lot of different things to people. It's what you make of it. But to say you hate Christmas. Who says that?"

Carli looked at her plate to avoid his gaze.

Nathan leaned in closer. "This is your first Christmas in Texas so join me and my family for lunch." He laid his arm around her shoulders. "You won't be sorry and, besides, I want you to be there."

"I'll think about it." How could she tell that handsome face no? This was going to be a much more difficult December than she ever imagined.

Chapter Six

Lank Torres left the cookhouse dining hall in a rush to finish up the day's work, or that's what he kept telling himself. There was still much to be done before the day was over, and he couldn't see any reason to linger over lunch so that everyone could keep telling him how sorry they were about his loss. By the time he got back on his horse, he was honest with himself. The real problem was Nathan Olsen was everything Lank was not. They had been friends since grade school, and Lank had always envied him.

Eldest born of a ranching legacy. One of the oldest and largest outfits in the area, and the one that Nathan would run someday. Brand new Silver Belly hat, custom-made chaps, alligator hide boots, handmade just for him no doubt. The Rafter O brand emblazoned on everything from his vest to his pickup truck.

And now Nathan Olsen had Carli's attention. Lank knew how he worked. Girls couldn't resist his charm and Hollywood good looks.

Lank reined his horse behind the keeper heifers, and, without saying a word, fell in next to Buck. A few of the other punchers had stayed to help drive them through a pasture across the road behind Carli's house, and up the fence line into the next pasture. They would stay there until next spring when a low-birth weight bull would be turned out with them.

He had noticed that Nathan left, and Carli never came out of the cookhouse. Washing dishes, he figured.

Lank forced himself to clear his mind and focus on the job at hand. Herding heifers was like trying to herd cats. Everything scared them, particularly men on horseback. They couldn't figure out which way to move. And if one broke from the group, they all went in the opposite direction. He rode ahead and opened the gate. They pushed them through and up a hill to the water tank and windmill where they were held for a while to let them calm.

After about fifteen minutes Buck circled his arm over his head and the cowboys turned their horses back down the hill and out the gate. They loped back to headquarters.

Buck reined close to Lank. "Remember, we're leaving for Dallas to see our niece and you're going to your sister's, right?"

"Maybe I should stay here?" Lank turned a frown to Buck.

"I think Carli can handle it. She's looking forward to it. We'll only be gone for a few days, and you'll just be in Amarillo. You can check on her, but, Lank, you need some time away."

"I guess," Lank said.

"You and your sister are still getting over your mother's passing. That takes time and the holidays are the worst. You should be with her. Go see those nephews."

Lank didn't want to talk about it, but he was dreading the holiday the closer it got to Christmas. And he couldn't stay here watching Carli and Nathan together. Why even consider that he might have a chance with her? Maybe some time away from this place was exactly what he needed.

They rode into headquarters and unsaddled. He skipped the gab sessions with the other punchers. Instead, Lank got the fences secured in the corral, tidied up the barn, and checked the feed bins so Carli would have enough for the week.

The sadness hung over him like a dark rain cloud. Spending all morning on the back of a horse hadn't pushed it away. He couldn't shake those last few days at the hospital when he sat by his mother's bedside. He wanted to remember the happier times, but those long days and nights still haunted him. She'd call out with pain in her sleep. The love she had in her eyes when she looked at him from a face he barely recognized, so thin and boney. Her breathing in shallow gasps. And all the things she wanted to tell him. She'd talked until she grew hoarse and weak. About marriage, how to cook tortillas, and stories about him as a baby.

He turned to open the gate for a few of the cowboys to pass through as they led their horses. Exchanged a few nods and waves goodbye. In a few short moments, everyone would be loaded and gone. The headquarters would be quiet until spring when they would all be back for roundup and branding. Buck appeared from out of the tack room.

"I can finish things up here. And then I think I will go on to my sister's. But if anything comes up, just let me know," Lank said.

"I plan to show Carli a few things before we leave. It should be a quiet week. Break ice if we get a cold spell, check salt and mineral blocks, nothing out of the ordinary. You know how quiet it is around here in December."

Lank nodded in agreement. "See you when you get back. Have a safe trip."

With that Lank turned to tidy up the tack room, sweep it out, and do a quick inventory of the meds stored in the saddle room fridge. At a loss to find anything else that would keep him at the corral, he wandered to his trailer house. He had hoped to catch a glimpse of Carli, but then decided he was too old for that kind of nonsense. She had him acting like a lovesick pup.

He should do laundry but decided to pack his dirty clothes instead. His sister wouldn't mind if he borrowed her washing machine. He was looking forward to seeing his nephews, Zane and Zachary.

Stuffing a pile of clothes from the floor into a garbage bag, he swung it into the back of his pickup truck. Made a pass to turn off lights, locked the door behind him, and drove through headquarters. He was not going to think about the new owner of the Wild Cow Ranch any longer. She couldn't do much better than his best friend Nathan. Maybe they were meant to be together. He wished them nothing but the best.

Chapter Seven

Saturday Afternoon, Shipping Day

"Say you'll come eat with us on Christmas Day." Nathan Olsen was persistent, and Carli couldn't think of any believable excuse to beg off. At least for the moment. Sliding out from under his arm that rested around her shoulders, she wished he would stop crossing into her space. But she had to admit, it was hard to resist him. She glanced around the cookhouse dining room at all the cowboys. Luckily, they were occupied with their plates of food, talking and not paying her any attention. She certainly didn't need any rumors circulating that she and Nathan might be a couple. Although he had made it more than obvious that he wanted nothing less.

"Are you done?" Carli reached for his plate. His hand went to her wrist.

"I'm not leaving the Wild Cow Ranch today until you say yes. Join me and my family at the Rafter O for lunch on Christmas Day. It will be one of the best days of your life. I promise."

She stacked his plate on top of hers. "I'll think about it."

"If I don't hear from you by Friday, I'm calling." He smiled in his mock bossiness. Again, irresistibly handsome.

She took the plates over to the wreck pan, and then sliced off two pieces of dessert and placed one in front of Nathan. "I'll let you know by Friday." Surely, she could think of a good reason by then to decline his invite. Christmas on top of a loud, boisterous family? No thanks.

Carli listened to Nathan chat about his new horse while they ate dessert. She halfway heard all about the famous Olsen family Christmas feast at the Rafter O Ranch, and told herself she wasn't going, even if she had to feign a headache. In the back of her mind, she worried about Lank and realized she'd been really insensitive to his loss. Thinking about how much she hated this time of year, but not even realizing the pain he must be going through having to spend the holiday without his mother. She made a promise to herself to find him later and apologize.

"I need to wash dishes for Lola. Thanks for helping us today with shipping, Nate." Several cowboys were stacking their plates on the cart, giving thanks to the cook, and heading towards the door. Carli expressed her gratitude to them as well.

"That's what neighbors are for, ma'am." Nathan winked as he walked over to the hat rack and placed his black felt cowboy hat on top of his six-foot frame. He made the perfect picture of a Texas cowboy. Carli studied him. His handsome face beamed with a smile directed right at her. "Call me if anything comes up this week. I remember Buck mentioned they're heading to visit their niece. I hope to hear from you on Friday." He tipped his hat and his spurs jangled as he walked out the door.

She smiled back and then turned to roll the wreck pan cart into the kitchen.

Suddenly the bustling cookhouse grew quiet. The cowboys would return in the spring for roundup and branding just like the grasses and sunflowers. She noticed Buck, her ranch foreman and Lola's husband, standing on the porch talking to a few of the dayworkers, Nathan being one of them.

"Lunch was delicious, Lola. Thank you." Carli parked the dirty dish cart next to the counter, dumped the soapy water from the wreck pan into the sink, and began putting silverware into the dishwasher.

"Thanks for your help. Normally I'd have plenty of time to clean up, but Buck and I would like to get out of here early in the morning. We have some packing to do before we can get on the road to our niece's home. I really appreciate your help with the dishes, Carli."

"Buck told me you were leaving. How long will you be gone?"

"We'll be home Saturday, on Christmas Eve. When we get back, I'd like for you to join us for dinner. Nobody should be by themselves on Christmas."

"It won't be the first Christmas I've spent alone, nor will it be the last. It's just a regular day to me."

Another invitation Carli cringed about but hid her feelings as she concentrated on the stack of dirty plates. Another meal where she'd have to smile and pretend she was having the best time of her life. No thanks. She enjoyed her solitary life more.

"How do you like my decorations?" Lola beamed at her as she wiped down the granite-topped island.

Carli cleared her throat and hesitated while she chose her words carefully. "Well, it looks like Christmas, that's for sure."

"This is my favorite holiday. You should go upstairs and take a look. I put a decorated tree in every bedroom, and miniature trees in the bathrooms."

"I'm not much on the commercialization. I've never put up a tree after the Fitzgeralds passed." Carli had no idea why she blurted out that bit of information. She rarely shared anything personal about her life with anyone. It had always been just her.

"They were the couple who raised you?"

"That's right."

"I have to say that makes me so sad, Carli. To think we had all those holidays here on the Wild Cow and you were in Georgia by yourself. I know it's Christian to forgive and forget but I'll never understand why your mother, Michelle, ran away and gave you up. And then kept you hidden from us."

"I used to think about her a lot, but now I just accept that as part of my past." Carli said. "It doesn't bother me much anymore."

"Your grandparents, Jean and Ward, loved this time of year. We started decorating on the day after Thanksgiving, and when it was all done, we hosted desserts and coffee during the first Sunday of every December. Friends and neighbors came to walk through the houses. We served hot apple cider and cookies. It took us almost a week to make enough cookies. Ward and Buck must have strung thousands of twinkle lights on all of the barns and fences. It was like a storybook, winter wonderland. For years, the fire chief always dressed as Santa. It was sad when he passed."

Carli focused on the sink full of soapy water as Lola rambled. She'd never known her grandparents nor would she ever meet any of the people that once lived here. There was no reason for her to even worry about past events. At some point she even felt immune to the stories. She had never been included in any of it.

She assured Lola more than once that she would finish cleaning up so that Lola could do her laundry and pack. She found the mop and bucket and began moving chairs away from the tables. After mopping the dining hall right quick, she planned on finding Lank to apologize. Guilt tugged at her. Of all people, she understood what holidays felt like without a mother, without family. It was impossible to ignore the cheerful energy of everybody around her, but it only made the loneliness worse. She knew all about being alone and tried convincing herself it was no big thing, but occasionally felt the twinge that she was different from the rest of the world.

Carli was dumping the dirty water into the utility room sink when Buck came in the back door.

"There you are. I need to give you a few instructions for next week if you have time."

"Just finished here, so this is perfect timing." Carli turned the bucket upside down in the sink to dry and followed Buck out to the corral.

Their boots crunched on the gravel drive as they walked to the pens. Guilt again nagged at her mind. "Do you know where Lank is?"

"He left. Went to visit his sister for a few days."

Disappointment hit her, and even more guilt. "When's he coming back?"

"Christmas Eve, I think. Are you sure you'll be all right here on your own?" Buck stopped and turned. "We can change our plans."

"Just tell me what you need me to do."

"I think the weather should be mild. Nothing unusual is predicted, so you'll only have to cake the cows a few times while we're gone. You need to do it every other day, unless a huge snowstorm moves in. I usually start on Monday. I'm leaving the feed truck keys in the console. Be sure to check the mineral blocks, and, when they get low, you'll find more stacked in one corner of the hay barn. If the temperature gets below freezing at night, you'll have to break the ice in their water troughs in the morning. Use the axe. It's in the feed truck, under the driver's seat."

Carli nodded and followed Buck through the corral and into the saddle house. She was looking forward to spending some time by herself on the ranch she had inherited. Since moving here, she was rarely alone. Diving headfirst into the work, she focused on learning everything she could. But there was still a lot she didn't know about a Texas cattle ranch.

Buck reminded her about the horse feed, which was kept dry and mouse-proof in metal containers. Carli already knew most of everything he went over, but she didn't interrupt. She had a lot of respect for this man who was so patient and kind, and who also had known her mother and grandparents. She wanted to talk to him more about that someday.

They walked out of the tack room. Her copper-colored horse, Beau, stood at the pipe rail, his neck stretched as far as he could. In the pen next to him, little Maverick, her bottle-fed calf, licked his nose.

Buck hovered at her elbow. "We're leaving first thing in the morning, and we'll be back before Christmas Eve, probably by mid-week. I don't want to be gone that long and leave you alone. If anything goes wrong, you can call Lola on her cell phone. Our niece's phone number and emergency numbers are on the bulletin board above the desk in the cookhouse."

At first Carli looked at him confused, and then stifled her grin. Obviously, he hadn't checked with his wife on when they were coming back because Lola had distinctly said it would be Saturday, Christmas Eve.

"We'll be fine, won't we?" Carli gave Beau a scratch between his ears. "What could possibly go wrong over a few short days?"

Chapter Eight

"She doesn't care a thing about me," he grumbled to himself as he drove out of the Wild Cow Ranch headquarters and turned onto the caliche county road. The new Miss High and Mighty Ranch Owner, Boss Lady, had spent most of lunch whining about not liking the holiday, never giving two cents about Lank or his problems. She only had eyes for the oldest Olsen brother. This was going to be a difficult holiday for him, so why did it matter what Carli thought?

He quibbled with himself, back and forth. Did she know about his mother? Or not? If she cared, she would have known what he was going through. Did she have a heart for others? Or was she spoiled, only thinking of herself and whatever issues she had about Christmas? He realized that she saw him as a ranch hand and that's what he'd always be. Spending his days in a saddle had been his only ambition since Ward had taken him on part-time after school. That had been over ten years ago, and he still loved every minute of his job.

He didn't have time for shallow girls. Sure, he was interested in her, but he didn't need the drama. The drama with her and Nathan Olsen. It would do him good to get away for a few days, spend time with his sister and her family. It had been just after the new year when they had lost their mother and he still thought about her. Oh, how he missed her. He was sure his sister did too.

The drive to Amarillo was under an hour. Lank was glad Kelly and her husband, Matt, had decided not to live in Houston where he grew up. They were close enough that Lank could be a part of his nephews' lives, especially since they were growing up so fast.

Lank's phone buzzed, and he hit the speaker button.

"Are you almost here, Lank? The boys are so excited." His sister's voice was tinged with her own electric energy. He could hear his nephews arguing in the background.

"As a matter of fact, I'm turning onto your street now."

Kelly and Matthew Reynolds lived in an older neighborhood with brick homes and stately trees, but with a lot of young families and kids. Neat, spacious yards and most were fenced. It was almost like a Norman Rockwell scene, as he drove down their street. Their two-story home was comfortable and full of happy, energetic times what with two boys running all over.

Matt had a good job as a computer programmer, and Kelly worked part-time as a real estate agent. Life was good for his sister, and he was glad. Most of the time. Except for the first of the year when

Lank and Kelly's mother was diagnosed with cancer.

But Lank didn't want to think of that time in their lives. He wanted to enjoy his nephews, his sister and her husband, and focus on the good things about this holiday season. If he could. His emotions fluctuated between extreme sadness, anger, and confusion as to why God took his mother away, and frustration about his own life and direction. And what about Carli? She seemed to creep into his mind more and more, usually when he least expected it. He may as well get over the new boss lady now.

His mother would have told him to pray about it. Pray about Carli. If she's the right one for you, you'll know it. Pray for Buck and Lola, and for your job. Pray for your sister. Lank had spent so much time praying at the bedside of his mother, he just didn't feel like he had any more prayers left in him.

Before he could even put the truck in park in their driveway, his nephews came running out of the house, screaming at the top of their lungs, "Uncle Lank! Uncle Lank's here!"

Kelly and Matt followed, all smiles. The boys anxiously jumped up and down at Lank's door. After turning the engine off, he unhooked his seatbelt and got out to greet them.

"Now, boys, settle down. Give Uncle Lank time to breathe. He just got here. Don't smother him," their mother gently chastised.

But there was no settling down. They squealed, jumped, hugged, pretty much clawed and climbed on Lank like he was a tree. He grabbed one under each arm and lifted them off the ground, which only produced more squeals.

"Now who have I got here? Zane or Zach? Are these really my nephews or some boys from down the street? What have you been feeding them?" He gave his sister a wide grin.

"We're your nephews! I'm Zane!" This from the six-year-old and he was a dynamo firing on all pistons. It would be hard to corral him.

The older one, only by a couple of years, waited a second for Zane to take a breath before he got close to Lank. Then with an earnest look he said, "Remember, Uncle Lank, you used to call me Little Matt, but I'm not so little anymore. Mom calls me Junior."

Lank looked to the mom and dad, smirked a little, but then regained his serious face. "Well, you have grown, haven't you, little man? Okay, I'll call you Junior if that'll work for ya." He extended his hand to shake on it, which visibly pleased Junior to no end. It almost appeared as if the boy grew another couple of inches after this exchange with his uncle.

Kelly and her husband greeted Lank, a tight hug from Kelly and a firm handshake from Matthew. "Welcome, man. Glad to have you. I'll get your bags."

"Only got the one. I'm not moving in." Lank laughed. "And it's full of dirty laundry. Can I borrow your washing machine, Sis?"

Kelly laughed and rolled her eyes. Matthew slapped him on the back. "Well, these boys might say something different if you asked them."

Whispering to Matt, Lank leaned in. "Just don't let them snoop under the tarp in the backseat. I've got a bunch of presents for them." Matt nodded.

Kelly placed an arm around Lank and they all headed in the house, the kids running like track stars to beat each other inside.

"Wow," Lank said as he saw the huge, heavily decorated Christmas tree by the front windows of the living room. "Kel, you're gettin' more like Lola. That is some tree."

His sister hugged her husband and smiled. "Well, everyone helped. Matthew and the boys. This is the biggest tree we've ever had. I decided that I'm tired of being sad." She looked at the little boys.

Zane was all ears and he jumped at Lank. "Uncle Lank, we made a really long list for Santa. We're gonna get so many cool things on Christmas morning. BB-guns, battery-operated cars, big ones we can drive! Video games, camo pants, maybe a playhouse for outside."

Junior interrupted. "It's a deer stand, dork, not a playhouse. Dad's gonna take us huntin'."

His father stepped in. "Didn't we talk about not calling your brother names?"

"Yes sir."

"And didn't we say we were going to discuss hunting?"

"Yes, sir."

"Now let's not ambush your Uncle Lank. Can you both please carry his bag to the guest room? I'm going to talk to your mom about dinner."

"Yes, sir."

Junior grabbed the bag to carry by himself as Zane struggled to hold onto part of it. "Let me carry some of it. Don't hog."

"I've got it. I can do it by myself." Junior tugged the bag away from his little brother.

"Boys." One word from their father was all it took for them to quiet down and stop their thrashing around.

Kelly came from the kitchen with a caffeine-free soda for Lank. She remembered. "Welcome to our world of wild boys."

"They're fine. Seems like they get bigger every time I see them," Lank said.

"I made a roast for dinner a little later. Is that okay?" Kelly said.

"I could take y'all out."

"No, you don't have to do that. Plus, it gets a little crazy sometimes with the boys in a restaurant. Although they are getting better."

"I think I'd like to shower before dinner. I kind of left the Wild Cow in a hurry."

"Sure. Take your time. Freshen up."

Alone in the guest room Lank's mind continued to reel. Even the hot shower didn't have the power to relieve his turmoil. Not only was his heart grieving the loss of his mother, but now he was questioning his future. He had always loved his work on the Wild Cow Ranch. Been there since he was a teenager. But where was he headed? Would he one day settle down like his sister had? Get married, have a family? Do all those things that people do. Like Nathan Olsen would most likely do. Maybe with Carli Jameson. It was obvious Nathan was setting his sights on her.

Lank held his head and rubbed his eyes. He had to make it stop. What did he care anyway about that girl from Georgia? She meant nothing to him. She was his boss. He would just focus on work and stop driving himself crazy with wonderings and what-ifs.

He took a deep breath and laid his head back on the pillow. Man, he was tired. Maybe just a little nap.

An hour later loud murmurs and scratches at his door entered his brain. Whispers of "Uncle Lank, you awake?" multiplied until he was fully awake, and they were not speaking in hushed tones any longer. "Uncle Lank, can we come in?"

He had to smile. Nothing like kids to take his mind off stupid adult issues. He needed to submerge himself in his nephews' activities, enjoy his sister and her husband's company, and try to embrace a new kind of Christmas without his mother. He stood and walked to the door.

Chapter Nine

Sunday, The Wild Cow Ranch

Most of Sunday morning was spent following Buck around again listening to instructions on how to fill the feeder bin on the pickup truck, pasture counts, and horse feed. How to break ice at every windmill using an axe without hitting yourself in the head or leg, and the locations of said mills. When Buck wasn't talking, Carli was reassuring him that everything would be fine.

"I can do this," she said for the tenth time. "Get out of here. Weren't you wanting to leave early? Go on. Your niece is expecting you."

"I just dread that Dallas traffic." Buck leaned against the corral fence like he didn't have a care in the world. "We do enjoy the Arboretum—so many beautiful plants and flowers, like a huge, manicured ranch—and, of course, Lola likes to walk through the Galleria. She's a thrifty shopper. Always wise with her dollars, looking for sales, and mostly enjoying the relaxing saunter through the stores but not really buying much. So, I can't complain."

"You need some time away. I've learned that ranch work is a 24/7 job. Cattle rarely care that it's a weekend." Carli walked towards the gate. Maybe Buck would follow. She imagined that Lola must be beside herself by now, wanting to hit the road.

"Are you sure you feel comfortable handling everything by yourself?" Buck asked her again.

"Yes, Buck. I've been living here awhile, followed you around as much as I could, and one week isn't that long. If I can't fill in when my employees need a few days off, then what good am I?"

Buck smiled and patted her shoulder. His eyes turned misty as he looked at her face. "Sure wish your grandparents were here to see this. You taking an interest in their place. You know, Christmas was a real big deal around here back then."

"That's what I understand from Lola."

"Everyone for miles around came to the Wild Cow Ranch during the holidays at one time or another. Your Grandpa Ward loved having company. The more, the better, he always said."

"I have to confess it's never been much of a celebration in my life. It's just another day, so you and Lola stay as long as you like. I'll be fine."

"You know, Carli, I understand some of what you're saying, I mean, about the hoopla of Christmas—the over-the-top decorations, Santa Claus, people feeling they have to spend a ton of money on gifts. It gets a little crazy if you ask me. I like to focus on the real meaning—the birth of Jesus. That's what it's about really. It all started in a dirty manger with smelly animals, kind of like where we put our stock sometimes if they're sick or laid up.

Here he was, a real king in heaven, and he humbled himself to come to earth, and be born as a human, for us. Do you ever think about that around Christmas?"

"Truthfully, not so much, Buck. I just wait for the season to be over with."

He turned a concerned frown to her and seemed as though he wanted to say more but didn't.

Later, with continued assurances and gentle nudges, Carli finally helped them load their SUV. It was already past noon. So much for an early start. She watched their taillights until they bumped over the cattle guard at the top of the hill and turned onto the county road. When they disappeared out of sight, she let out a sigh of relief. All she had to do was run the cookie wagon on Monday and Wednesday, break ice if it got below freezing during the night, and then Buck would take care of everything when he got back.

Carli planned to ride her horse, Beau, every single day. He still needed an introduction to cattle work. She'd take him through the heifers. They were always so jumpy and cautious; it would be good practice for him. All her training with horses told her that patience and repetition were the important ingredients to success.

Once, in Atlanta, she had watched a demonstration by the Mounted Police. Those horses had to be ready for anything around downtown—crowds, gunshots, car backfires, water hoses or hydrants, you name it. One officer opened and closed an umbrella very close to a horse's face and explained how they must've practiced with it a hundred or more times, but now the horse could care less. The piéce de résistance was when the patrol drove heavy construction equipment near the horses, complete with loud, rumbling motors and backup beeps and whistles, and buckets that lifted high above the horses' heads—normally, one of the number one fears for equines, but these horses just stood nonchalant as though they were about to take a nap. Sure, they watched the equipment, but they didn't spook or get worried. Why? They had done this a hundred times or more.

That's all Carli had to do, practice and show Beau patience and tell him the heifers were no big deal. She would turn this show horse into a fine ranch horse, she just knew it.

Genealogy research was also on her agenda this week. Her birth father's name appeared on a birth certificate she discovered in her grandparents' house, the house where she now lived. There were cabinets and dresser drawers stuffed full, stacks of boxes in the basement yet to be sorted through. In many ways she felt intrusive going through their belongings even though it was her stuff now. Her Grandpa Ward had changed his Last Will only a month before he died, leaving everything to her but he hadn't lived long enough to meet her. It took the lawyers some time to track Carli down. Buck told her the man had spent a good part of his life trying to find her.

Michelle, her mother, was a pregnant, teenaged runaway and had discarded the burden of raising her child, choosing instead a life unencumbered and free. Carli knew very little about where she went or who she had been. It comforted her somewhat knowing that Ward and Jean, her grandparents, Michelle's parents, had tried to find her. Buck told her they never gave up hope of bringing their only grandchild back to the Jameson family ranch.

Interestingly enough, both Jean and her mom had kept the family name, Jameson. And Carli's guardians, the Fitzgeralds, had never officially adopted or changed her name. She kept the name she was born with, Carlotta Jean Jameson. And then they'd kept her hidden her whole life, but why? So many unanswered questions. Answers she would never know or understand. She thought about those past Christmases and the family times she never was a part of. Her heart ached. The time gone, she could never go back. Why hadn't she searched for them when she got older, after the Fitzgeralds passed and she was on her own? She had been by herself for so long, it never occurred to her that life could be anything different.

Her life in Georgia had been pleasant and set in place. She focused on her horses, the competitions, and her clients, pouring everything she had into horse training with her business partner, Mark, who ended up upset with her over the whole Texas thing. And she immersed herself into the horse show circuit and then a boyfriend, Josh. She really thought he was the one, and fell fast and completely, but he dumped her after only a few months. When he kissed her cutthroat competitor at the Georgia International Horse Park, that was the first clue he and Carli were over. Alone again. Everyone left. Nothing new. This next time, if there ever was a next time, she would be more cautious before getting involved with anyone. Particularly any Texas cowboys.

As she walked back to the house, Carli imagined

a roomful of people celebrating Christmas. The smells and sounds of past parties. She imagined the ache that must have consumed Jean and Ward, knowing their only granddaughter and daughter were out there somewhere. Carli had been loved unconditionally but never knew it.

Michelle did name the father on the birth certificate which at least gave Carli a place to start. Somewhere out there she had another family. If Michelle was only sixteen at the time, she found herself pregnant, it stood to reason the boy might've been local. Maybe he was alive and well, living right here in the area.

Carli was nervous, but excited too about what she might find. Growing up with no family, Carli was grateful the Fitzgeralds had been kind, but they were elderly and consistent homebodies. They had their habits like watching "Jeopardy" every night. She considered herself lucky that they encouraged and supported her love of horses, but they rarely came to her shows, instead, dropped her off at the lesson barn where all the kids would go to the horse shows as a group. Again, left to her own devices. And some of the barn girls from wealthier families were cliquish so it was hard to make friends.

She always dreamed of belonging to a big family with aunts and uncles and cousins. People who genuinely wanted her around, others she felt a kinship with. Maybe she had a half-brother or half-sister out there? That would be interesting. She hoped they would accept her, but buried this hope deep within, protected.

Now she had a new life in Texas. And she might have a father out there too. She hoped. A father. Too afraid to say the word aloud for fear that he was another part of her that she'd never be able to find, to hold onto.

Chapter Ten

Sunday evening, Range Riders Arena

After church and Sunday lunch, Lank waited until Kelly put his nephews down for a nap and then he left for a charity roping at the Range Riders Arena. It saved a lot of begging and crying on the boys' part and a lot of guilt for him. They were a handful for sure. He would have to make it up to them later when they woke up and discovered he had left without them.

His mood lightened and he smiled at the sight of parked pickup trucks and trailers bursting out of the lot all the way from the arena to the road. He had to park in the bar ditch. He wouldn't be competing this year, only watching and offering encouragement. Roping had never been his favorite. The life of following the rodeo circuit still called to him but he hadn't the nerve to answer.

Riding broncs was the one thing he had given up for his mother when she was alive. The sport fed his restless spirit, and he loved every minute until he suffered a bad concussion in Fort Worth which brought his mother to tears. She never left his side the whole time he was in the hospital. He could have made it to the NFR, everybody who should know had said so. That injury had cost him a career in Pro Rodeo.

"Lank. Glad you made it, man." His best friend and running buddy since high school, Colton Creacy, gave him a wide grin. "This is Pamela."

Of course, Colton would have the most beautiful girl who happened to be the rodeo queen at his side. Lank offered his hand and said hello.

She returned the greeting with a dazzling smile, fully aware of the captivating picture she made. Head to toe queen material with every blonde hair in place from under a purple cowboy hat. Instead of a leather hat band, a blinding tiara. Her western shirt glittered with rhinestones and the satin white "Queen" banner hung from one shoulder, emblazoned across her body.

"You're staying for the dance after, aren't ya?" Colton asked.

"Sure," said Lank. He had nothing better to do.

"See you there," said Pamela as she leaned forward and gave him a peck on the cheek.

Colton shot him a thumbs up behind her back. Lank ignored his friend and found a seat in the stands. He made it just in time for the grand entry.

The announcer explained that all proceeds from the team entry fees, concessions, and donations would go to the cancer wing at the children's hospital in Amarillo. In one part of the stands, sat the families of those kids and if they were able, the kids themselves. They all wore bright lime green T-shirts with Stronger Than Cancer printed across the front, some with bandanas on their hairless heads.

The roping teams rode into the arena, a header and a heeler each wearing matching shirts. Loping once around the arena, then lining up down the middle. Next, Queen Pamela with the American flag and the younger Junior Miss Rodeo carried the Texas flag. As the crowd stood to sing, they rode around and around the arena while the National Anthem played.

The first team came out and had a good calf that ran straight out of the chute. The header sent a beautiful loop that landed on the horns, turned the calf so that the heeler could come in behind, but missed the hind feet with his loop. No time.

Colton was next, his partner one of his buddies from a neighboring town. Lank didn't know him that well, but he was a good cowboy. He had helped them at the Wild Cow on occasion. Colton burst out of the pocket and did his job, turned the calf, and the heeler caught both hind legs but suddenly grabbed his hand and lost the dally. Colton had to hang on to his rope as he followed the calf to the far end of the arena, and they all went out the gate. Lank couldn't tell what had happened.

He watched the next few teams, and then thought about getting something to drink. Making his way through the stands, and just as he jumped to the ground Colton rushed up in a panic.

"I need a partner. Mike snapped his fool thumb off. You have to heel for me. You can use his horse."

"I'm not a roper."

"I've seen you rope plenty times."

"That's part of my job, when a calf or cow needs to be doctored. Or when I have to catch a horse. This is timed."

"Just pretend you're at the Wild Cow doing your job and you'll do fine. I can't go home after only one go-round."

Colton had gotten him out of a jam more than once. Lank hung his head. "Oh, good grief."

"Thanks, man. I owe ya."

"You're darn right you owe me," Lank said, but Colton had already dashed off into the crowd before he could finish the sentence. Lank hurried to catch up.

Since it wasn't an official PRCA event and just for charity, Lank had no problem subbing for Mike. He had to adjust the stirrups and had just settled into the saddle when they were called to get ready. Colton backed into the pocket and Lank settled his horse on the other side of the chute. The buzzer went off.

Colton roped the horns and swung the calf around so that his hind feet were exposed to Lank. He hesitated a minute, swung the rope over his head several more times than he should have, but hit the mark. They stretched the calf out for a few seconds between them to stop the clock. The time wasn't the fastest, but it was decent.

Colton nodded his appreciation. Lank felt good to be in the arena with the crowd cheering, the heavy breaths of the livestock, the dust hanging in the air. Actually it felt more than good. That mind-body-spirit connection. This is where he belonged.

Maybe he should take up something like roping

or bulldogging. Both were fun sports and might be a little easier on his injured brain. He considered that promise made to his mother almost ten years ago. So, what if he got hurt again? Nobody cared and at least he'd go out on top doing what he loved.

The remainder of the go-rounds went well. They didn't have the winning time, but they had an acceptable showing. Colton was happy with third place and a new buckle. After the awards were handed out, they swung up into the saddle one more time for the grand finale. The winning team rode several times around the area, waving as the crowd cheered. The rodeo queens brought the flag around again and the roping teams filed in and lined up in the middle.

Lank noticed a small child with a balloon stand up on the front row. Time stood still in the next few minutes as Lank envisioned the wreck that was about to happen, but there was nothing he could do. Just as the kid walked closer to the railing, Pamela and her horse made a wide circle and came down close to the stands. A breeze caught the balloon and pushed it right into the horse's line of sight and that's when the animal went haywire. The horse skidded to a stop and jumped straight up several times. Pamela lost the grip on the flag but stayed on her horse. The flag fell into the stands. And then her horse tore out like his tail was on fire. Lank spurred his horse and took off after her. He cut the corner short and caught up to them on the other side of the arena where he steered his horse alongside her.

"I got ya," he said.

Colton rode up on the other side and reached for the reins.

Pamela leaned closer to Lank, wrapped her arms around his waist, and he eased her out of the saddle. She slid gently to the ground and then bent over at the waist, her sides heaving. Lank jumped to the ground beside her.

"Are you hurt?"

"No."

Colton appeared with her horse, which she got on, and they all three rode out of the arena as the crowd cheered. As soon as they were through the alley, Pamela reined up and looked at Lank.

"What happened?" she asked.

"A balloon. I'm glad you're not hurt," he said. He stepped out of the saddle, and she did the same, standing next to him.

"Thank you," she said, unshed tears glistened in her eyes. And then she leaned in and planted a warm, wet kiss on his mouth. "See you at the dance. I've got to go find my flag."

"It's in the stands. At least you didn't let it touch the ground," said Colton. He gave her a cocky grin and then shot Lank a mean glint.

Pamela led her horse away.

"That's my queen," Colton said.

Lank laughed. Colton called dibs on all the queens and any other girls he'd meet before the night was done. That guy would never settle down.

"I'm leaving. Have fun. Are you taking Mike's horse? Is he still at the hospital?"

"Bring him to my trailer for now. I'm sure Mike will send someone to get his horse and rig."

As Lank drove away he thought of Pamela and that kiss, but he had no desire to turn around. The rodeo queen's face kept getting replaced by the girl from Georgia who now called Texas home. He had it bad and he knew it.

Chapter Eleven

Sunday

By the time Buck and Lola pulled out of the Wild Cow headquarters, it was way past noon. It would take them five or more hours to get to Dallas, depending on road construction and traffic.

Lord, help me to cool down during that time.

Lola was more than a little annoyed with Buck. They had talked about leaving early, maybe six a.m., and get to Dallas in time to have lunch with their niece, Rena.

That wasn't going to happen now. It'd be more like dinner time when they arrived, maybe even after dark. All because Buck couldn't let go of his responsibilities at the Wild Cow. He must've gone over chore instructions with Carli ten times each. He had been gone most of the morning.

Lola figured Carli might also have been annoyed with Buck for his over-the-top thoroughness and repetitive directions. It might've seemed like Buck didn't trust Carli to do simple chores like feed the stock. Lola knew Carli was up to the challenge. She'd been living at the Wild Cow Ranch awhile and had watched Buck and Lank numerous times as they completed their tasks. Plus, she had a history with horses. That had to count for something even if she didn't know everything about cows.

The car was quiet as Buck drove. Lola felt she should break the tension but wasn't sure what she wanted to say. She was still miffed at him. They'd missed church. If she had known they would be leaving so late, Lola could have gone to early church even if Buck couldn't make it.

That man!

As Lola was taking in deep breaths and letting out slow sighs, Buck suddenly stopped the car and pulled to the side of the road.

"We should pray before getting on the interstate."

Lola's anger melted a little and she felt ashamed.

Buck took her hand and held it tightly. He started the prayer.

"Lord, please be with us on this trip. Keep us safe on the road and bring us back home in one piece. We thank you for giving us this time off from work and ask you to please bless us and renew our minds and bodies. Let us be a blessing to our niece Rena and help her in any way that we can."

Lola mumbled, "Yes, Lord."

"Please give Lola and me a special time together as husband and wife. We don't always get that time at home when we're so busy with the ranch. Please watch over and protect Carli as she takes care of the Wild Cow by herself this week. Thank you for my time with Carli earlier when I tried to share with her the real meaning of Christmas. And Lord, let us shine Your light to all that we meet along our journey."

That man could say a prayer that went right to the core of her soul. His voice always revived her spirit. Before he could say, "Amen" Lola squeezed his hand and added to the prayer.

"And Lord, please cleanse me of any resentment. Let me forgive Buck for what I perceived as our lateness in heading out on our trip this morning. You must've had another plan for Buck to share that time with Carli. Help me to go with the flow and not be selfish. And yes, thank you Lord, for making this trip possible for us. May we have a wonderful time. In Your name. Amen."

Before starting the engine, Buck placed both hands on Lola's and said, "Sorry, Hon, for causing us to be late this morning. Carli and I had a good talk about Christmas. I really felt led to share with her about that. She's so mixed up about the holiday. But I want you to know that I love you with all my heart and I'm looking forward to spending these days with you, and Rena. I want you to have a wonderful time. We can do whatever makes you happy—shopping, botanical garden, restaurants." He smiled, then reached out to give her a big hug.

"That was a nice prayer, Buck. How can I stay mad at you? I know that you'd rather be out in the middle of a lake somewhere fishing and that a big city is the last place you want to be, but I am glad you're going with me. Now let's get this trip started. I want to shop till we drop!"

His eyes bulged wide, and he moaned. She added, "Don't worry. There are stores out there waiting on me, and I'm sure there's a bench with your name on it."

"I love you, Lola."

"I love you too. Now put the pedal to the metal."

Rena's little white house was in an older neighborhood of the Dallas suburbs. Near an historic district, she could walk to a coffee shop but it also bordered a known crime area, so she was vigilant about safety. Her mother was Lola's sister and the two frequently talked about Rena living on her own. But she was near thirty and had already had some not so favorable roommate experiences. Her job as a first-grade teacher was going well but she couldn't afford to buy a house. This rental would have to do for now.

Lola had called ahead to tell Rena of their delay and now that they had arrived in her driveway, Lola's excitement was nearly bubbling over. It had been over a year since they had seen their niece.

Rena was waiting on the porch to greet them. Lola opened her car door and nearly forgot to unhook her seat belt.

"Rena!"

"Aunt Lola!"

The two women ran into each other's arms and held on tightly. Buck had stopped the car and came around for his hug.

"Rena, girl. You're looking good."

"Oh, Uncle Buck. It's so good to see you both."

He held her in his strong arms. This was the daughter he and Lola never had. They had prayed for and known her since before she was born. She was so special to them.

"Let's get your luggage inside. You must be tired from the drive."

Lola ran her fingers through her hair. "Well, I guess we are. It took a little longer than we thought. Six hours instead of five. There was construction and traffic around the city."

As Buck carried the suitcases, Rena helped with some of the bags as Lola described their contents. "I made you some of your favorite carrot-cranberry muffins. And I also have banana nut bread. And fixings for whole wheat blueberry pancakes tomorrow morning."

Rena interrupted. "Did you bring the kitchen sink, Aunt Lola?"

Buck laughed. "You know your aunt, Rena girl. Always prepared."

As they got inside and unloaded packages on the kitchen counter, Rena announced, "I've made some dinner for us. I figured after your long drive we wouldn't want to go out tonight. We'll just relax and catch up."

"Oh, I didn't want you to go to any trouble for us, Rena." Lola's face turned sad, but her niece wouldn't let that be the tone for the evening.

"Aunt Lola, please let me spoil you a little. You and Uncle Buck always do so much for me—sending packages, cards, and money I might add. Tomorrow we can do whatever you want, and we'll have lunch."

"Our treat!" Lola was quick to jump in.

"All right, your treat. If I can't stop you."

"Right, Buck? Our treat."

Buck fiddled with his phone again. "I think I

should check on Carli. I'm just gonna step outside." It was about the fifth time he had said it since they had left the Wild Cow. Or maybe the tenth. Lola had lost count.

"Now, Buck, don't make me take that phone away from you. Carli is just fine. You don't need to check up on her." Lola's hands were on her small hips. That was never a good sign. "We haven't been gone for even a day."

Rena grinned and Buck resigned himself to sit on a kitchen barstool as the women gabbed and flitted around.

"Here's some cheese and crackers to tide you over." Lola put a plate in front of Buck and went back to asking Rena about what she had cooked for dinner.

"I thought maybe you'd like salmon burgers. But if not and you want meat and potatoes then I also have meatloaf, mashed potatoes, and salad. Your choice. I made both."

"Well, I know Buck'll like the meatloaf, but I'd like to try the salmon burgers." While a sweet gesture, Lola wondered why she'd made two different dinners. Her niece was always overeager to please.

The women continued their banter and Buck munched. Lola stole glances at him. She had a strong feeling he was doing his best not to think of the ranch or Carli. She had to get his mind off them if she could. But if there's one thing years of marriage had taught her, she had absolutely no control over her strong Texas man. He did what he wanted which is why she was even more grateful that he was sitting beside her on this trip.

"Rena, how are things going with you? Job, friends. Any dating?"

"Aunt Lola, please don't worry about me. I'm doing okay. I did find a church. I go to a Bible study every Wednesday night. I've made some friends. But no one I'd be interested in dating. It's hard when you get to my age. The thirty-year-old guys want to date twenty-year-olds."

"Buck, what do you think? Why don't you give us the male perspective?" Lola's effort to include him in their conversation resulted in an annoyed glare.

Buck popped another cheese and cracker into his mouth. But Lola was not going to let him escape. She glared right back at him.

With a half full mouth, he said, "Aw, ladies, I don't know what makes people tick. Rena, I'd advise you to guard your heart. Don't give in to the temptations of the world or fall for some jerky guy's tricks. Stay strong. Pray hard. God will bless you and give you the desires of your heart. Lola and I are always praying for you, sweety."

"I know you are, Uncle Buck. And I really appreciate it. And love you both. That's enough about me. Don't you have a new boss at the Wild Cow? I was sorry to hear about Ward's passing."

While they ate dinner, Lola brought her up to speed on the changes at the ranch. "You should meet Carli. She's very independent like you and she hasn't found her guy either. One thing for certain, I'm glad I don't have to worry about dating these days."

"You caught yourself a good one," said Rena.

Buck grinned and helped himself to peach pie. As Rena poured the coffee, Lola became as animated as a kid going to the circus the next day.

"So, tomorrow we'll head to the Galleria for some mega shopping?" Her smile was ear to ear. "And there's a little antique shop I'd like to stop at."

"Aunt Lola, you'll love the Galleria. I can't remember the last time you went. They still have the ice-skating rink and they put a giant Christmas tree in the middle this time of year. It's all so pretty. Really gets you in the Christmas spirit."

Lola watched Buck who didn't have the happiest expression on his face.

"Yes, Rena, and we could use some Christmas cheer to help us relax, get our minds off work." Then pointedly she said, "We work so hard, especially Buck. It's a lot of responsibility running the Wild Cow Ranch."

"You have that new owner now though. Can't she run things while you're away?"

"That's just it. Buck's worried about leaving Carli on her own for this whole week while we're gone. He's afraid something will happen."

Buck frowned. "She doesn't know squat about a cattle operation. Wonder if the weather changes? Anything could happen."

Rena touched Buck's arm that rested on the counter. "Uncle Buck, you always taught me that we shouldn't worry or be anxious. Jesus said that, right? You said to give our troubles to God. Can you do that? Give your worries about Carli and the ranch to God?"

Buck looked at his sweet niece. "How'd you get so smart?"

"I take after my aunt," Rena replied.

Chapter Twelve

Monday, Day 1 Alone

Carli stretched, snuggled under her cushy comforter for one more minute, and listened to the birds' serenade. The first rays of light cast a glow on her window and peeked through the sheer curtains. She was more than a little excited. Everything that happened over the next few days would depend entirely on her. She was totally and ultimately in charge of the Wild Cow Ranch. Her ranch. But she really knew nothing about these people or cattle ranching. Life could throw some strange curve balls at times.

As she stepped off the front porch into the sunshine, she closed her eyes and drew in a deep cleansing breath. The kind of breath Lola had taught them to do in yoga class. Filling her core with air, tightening her muscles to exhale. When she opened her eyes, she froze. Blinked. Shut her eyes again to convince her brain she hadn't seen what she had just seen. Slowly opening her eyes again, yep, the vision was real all right. As she stepped off the porch, her boot sank into something soft. Even if her eyes had fooled her, her nose told her it was an animal by the smell coming from her boot. "Good grief!"

A cow. To be more exact, a black and white dairy cow stood in her front yard chewing on the grass. And the poor girl's pink udder was stretched to the bursting point. The animal lazily raised its head and looked in Carli's direction. A swirl of white etched her face trailing to a large black nose. Soft black eyes framed by fluttery eyelashes, her face showing no concern for danger, so she returned to munching on the dry, winter grass.

Carli stared at the four-legged visitor for a few minutes, reasoning that this is a cow so obviously she must need her horse. She would put the bovine in the corral and then call the sheriff. Surely someone would report a missing animal. Had to belong to one of her neighbors, she figured.

In no time, Carli had Beau saddled and rode him to the corral. Hopping off his back, she held the gate open with a horseshoe welded to a chain. Her plan was to drive the cow right through the opening where it would be away from the road and close to the water trough. Easy-peasy. Cowboys did it all the time. She trotted Beau across ranch headquarters to her front yard. Carli wanted to pat herself on the back for figuring out a solution all on her own. She could definitely run this ranch. How hard could it be?

Except this dairy cow was in no way the slightest bit intimidated by a cowgirl on a horse. File that under information she never knew before. They circled and Carli yelled, swinging her rope, but nothing happened. The cow only took a few steps forward, grazing along the way, then stopped at a new patch of winter grass.

"Let's go. Yay! Yay! Move along, girl!"

Beau seemed to be trying to listen and fulfill Carli's commands. He had always been a good student for anything she wanted to teach him. She remembered when she first practiced with him to go over a little bridge for an upcoming horsemanship class. At first, he was unsure, his horseshoes clunking across the wood, but in short order he walked back and forth across that bridge as though it was old hat to him.

And now he wasn't afraid of this full-sized cow in any way. So, he complied with whatever direction Carli pointed him in. Maybe he wasn't certain of her entire plan, but at least he was cooperative.

After a good half-hour of making no progress whatsoever, a thought suddenly occurred to her. She slid off Beau and made a large loop with her rope. Walking towards the cow with soft steps, she spoke gently, "There now, easy, girl." Pretty as you please, she walked up to the cow and slipped the loop right over her head. Carli tugged and the milk cow followed. Wow, who knew this would work?

Carli led her across the gravel drive and right into the pen. Great! Like walking a big dog. Slipping the rope off and shutting the gate behind her, she went back to get Beau. Looping Beau's reins around the porch rail, she quickly ran inside to grab her cell phone and call the sheriff.

By the time she had Beau unsaddled and the tack back in its place, the sheriff's cruiser pulled slowly into ranch headquarters and stopped next to the pens. Carli waved when he unfolded himself out of the slicktop, black Tahoe that displayed his elected title spelled out in bright gold letters along the side.

"Sheriff Anderson. Thanks for coming out."

"Carli." He tipped his Silver Belly Stetson in her direction and placed both hands on his gun belt before walking towards her with a confident swagger. Sheriff Anderson wasn't Hollywood handsome, but he had a strong jaw and exuded that take-charge attitude that most law enforcement officers have. He made her feel better just by being there.

"I have a problem, Sheriff. I found that standing in my front yard this morning." She gestured with her open palm, and both their heads turned to look at the speckled beast who stood at the water trough. The sound of long slurps drifted towards them in the peaceful morning.

"A cow?" Sheriff Anderson turned his head around to look everything over, pushed his hat back, and scratched the top of his forehead. "Carli, this is a cattle ranch. Cows are not that unusual around here."

She looked at him and he stared back for several seconds until Carli broke the silence. "It's a milk cow. Do you know who it might belong to?"

"Normally, people report missing livestock. I rarely get calls about new acquisitions."

"So, what should I do?"

"Well, I guess you could start by contacting your neighbors and asking around. See if anyone is missing a dairy cow."

"I might remember some of their names, but not

all. And I don't have their contact information. The only number I could find posted on the bulletin board in my kitchen was yours."

"You called my private cell phone. Oh, that's right. Buck's gone this week. He mentioned it and asked that I check on you. How long has he been gone?"

"He and Lola left yesterday after lunch."

The sheriff laughed. "It hasn't even been twenty-four hours yet, and you're already calling me? I'd say you've got things well in hand, so carry on. If anyone reports a missing milk cow, I'll be sure to let you know. Just keep her water bucket filled and you might give her some cow cake, same stuff you're feeding the herd. And I'm sure you've noticed, she needs to be milked. Probably in some pain. I've got to go check on a break-in. Have a good week, Carli."

She hated the thought of the poor thing being in pain, and she was a tad aggravated that he had to point out the obvious. Of course, she would give the poor dear water and feed. Carli held her tongue and stood silent.

Sheriff Anderson turned before getting back into his vehicle. "Seriously though, save my private cell for emergencies only, if you don't mind. Feel free to call the office number anytime."

"Thanks again, Sheriff." Carli watched him drive away. Obviously, a burglar was way more important than her livestock predicament, and it seemed he couldn't get away fast enough.

"Whatever you say, Sheriff," Carli mumbled to herself, and she couldn't help but feel a bit foolish.

He left her with, "Have a good week," which probably meant he didn't want to hear from her again. She turned to look at the black and white cow that seemed oblivious to the trouble it had caused, and for the life of her, not one neighbor's name came to Carli's mind. She hurried inside to search YouTube videos on how to milk a cow.

Chapter Thirteen

Monday, Mid-morning

With rope in one hand and a bucket in the other, Carli made a determined beeline to the corral and the dairy cow that stood in the pen watching her. Confident after intense study in the art of cow milking, she worried that the bulging udder was painful and that the animal might be suffering.

She set the bucket down and walked with easy, cautious steps towards the bovine. As before, the cow did not mind the rope going over her head and she followed Carli to the other side of the pen. Carli tied her next to the fence feeder now filled with fresh hay, and the cow buried her nose in the straw and munched away.

Carli took a warm rag from the clean bucket, and, as instructed on the video, wiped down the udder and teats. The cow swished her tail and raised one foot. Obviously, she might be a little sore. Just wiping down the teats caused milk to dribble on the ground, making Carli think she might have been wandering around for several days missing milking time.

Next, the bucket was placed under the cow and Carli couldn't help but be excited as she contracted her fingers as was shown on the video. White liquid in narrow streams began to fill the bucket. She didn't have to squeeze that hard because the udder was so full. One hoof suddenly drew up and overturned the bucket spilling its contents on the ground. Carli rinsed out the milk and dirt at the water faucet and returned to her chore.

Before long she had a half-full bucket, and the udder was considerably smaller. She kept working until the liquid almost reached the brim. Not sure what to do with the milk, she filled the barn cats' dishes, and they came running from their hiding places as if their secret cat radar had sounded an alarm. The rest she took over to her house and poured into sterilized containers, covered, and placed them in the refrigerator. Her orphaned bull calf Maverick might enjoy a bottle or two. She thought about trying a glass that night with her dinner.

Returning to the corral, she slipped the rope from around the dairy cow's neck and watched her finish the hay. A sense of accomplishment filled her. With that chore done she needed to go into town for a few groceries. Tomorrow she would start contacting the neighbors in hopes of locating the home of the wayward dairy cow.

Even though it was the dead of winter, the little town of Dixon reminded her of a lazy summer day. No one was in a rush, traffic moved along at an excruciating pace, much slower than she would have liked, and everyone she passed raised an arm in greeting. At first, she had resisted, but now did the same. After moving here, she soon learned that everyone knew who she was even though she didn't know a soul. Jean and Ward's long-lost granddaughter was found and as the only heir, new owner of the Wild Cow Ranch. It still felt strange how everyone called her by name.

Turning into the parking lot for Roy's Grocery, she made a mental note to treat herself by stopping in the coffee shop on the way out of town. An unusually large bunch of jingle bells hanging from the door frame rang out as she stepped inside the grocery. A small mannequin Santa suddenly came to life, swaying his hips from side to side and blurting out Here Comes Santa Claus.

The young checkout girl turned to her with a wide smile and called out over the singing Santa, "Welcome to Roy's. Me-e-e-rry Christmas!" If the elongated "Merry" wasn't enough, the clerk wore a bright green T-shirt with sparkling red letters that read, Our Balls are Jingling. Carli was stunned to silence and couldn't help but stare at the girl's shirt.

"It's a typo." Julie with the name tag laughed. "It's supposed to say 'Bells,' but Roy got them really cheap because of the misprint. We have a bunch on hand for our customers too if you want one."

"I'm good, but thanks." Recovering from the

joyful greeting, Carli shrank even more as she gazed around the store. Oh, how she hated red and green. Just like the cookhouse at her ranch, it was a Christmas explosion. Only for a few seconds during the peaceful morning, she had completely forgotten about the time of year until now. She doubted she could find one empty surface or space that didn't have holiday decorations.

To her immediate right was a tower of boxes made with the bright red of Coca Cola and the lime green of Sprite. To her immediate left, a colorful wall of candy. Every kind you could imagine from giant plastic tubes full of jellybeans to a low table covered in stacks of chocolate bars and Bazooka bubble gum. A shelf underneath the table held a rainbow of glass bottled drinks. Baskets on the floor held pixie sticks and jaw breakers. Overhead, white paper snowflakes and candy canes swayed as far as the eye could see. Carli's heart pounded in her chest, and, without saying a word, she simply turned around and left.

It took several moments in the pickup to catch her breath and calm her heart. She couldn't explain why this time of year set her into a drowning pool of anxiety, but it always did. Maybe it was of her own making, or maybe it was a trauma that had long since been forgotten. Mostly it was the aggravation of so much stuff and people and more stuff. Regardless, the bigness of the season overwhelmed her, as though she was sinking in some Christmas village nightmare. With a few deep breaths, she backed out of the parking lot and drove across Main Street to the other grocery store. The owner was a brother of Roy's, and she parked in front of

Jack's Grocery, or as Lank called it, Grumpy Jack's.

Carli felt peace and calm the minute she walked through the door. Not a Christmas tree in sight and the elderly clerk behind the even more ancient cash register barely glanced up from her magazine. Sunlight streaming through the front window cast light on the sparkling dust particles that floated in the air. Carli finished her shopping in peace.

"You're Ward and Jean's granddaughter, aren't you?" The clerk watched Carli pile the items on the counter.

"Yes, I am."

"How long you staying for this time?"

Not that it was any of her business. "Actually, I've moved here permanently. I'm living in their house at the Wild Cow Ranch."

"We sure do miss them."

As the clerk rang up her purchases, Carli just happened to remember her new furry guest.

"You wouldn't happen to know anybody who lives out that way that might own a dairy cow, would you?"

"No, can't say that I do. No one comes to mind. The Wilsons own goats, make homemade soaps and cheese. We got a variety over there if you want to try some. The Browns run a sheep herd and..."

Carli barely listened to the rattling of names and ongoing list of livestock inhabiting the county. She just wanted to find the owner of that cow. By the time she had written out a check for her groceries—because as the clerk explained, "Jack refuses to pay credit card fees to those feather-headed corporate swindlers,"—Carli really needed that coffee with a double shot of espresso as soon as possible.

She swung her grocery bags into the back and hopped into her truck, barely slowing down at the four-way stop to turn into the coffee shop.

Belinda, one of the owners and the "B" of B&R Beanery and Buns, smiled at her from behind the bar. "Where have you been, girl?"

"Tending to grandpa's cows." Carli laughed. One glance around the coffee shop told her she would be able to relax for a minute. Decorations were minimal, and the smell of roasting coffee beans radiated warmth and happiness all the way through, clean down to her toes. Best of all no holiday tunes, just soft rock turned low coming from the sound system. She couldn't contain the grin that spread over her face.

Belinda laughed. "You are just in time to try my newest creation—"

Carli held up a hand to stop her. "Hold it. Nothing to do with Christmas, please."

"Okay. Hmm, let me think." Belinda turned to her menu board. "I've got it. Something warm, with a double shot of go-juice. How about a cinnamon French toast latte? Large, of course."

"Bring it on." Carli watched her new friend. This had certainly become one of her favorite places in the little town of Dixon. It wasn't the upscale, big city vibe of the espresso bar she had frequented in Georgia, but the smells were the same. Belinda and her husband roasted their own beans. And as an added bonus, Belinda turned out to be a really good listener and friend.

"I remember the first time you came in here. A brand-new heiress of a Texas ranch. You seemed so lost. I felt bad about having to close early and leave for soccer that day, but that's life in a small town. It's a blessing we're able to build our work schedule around our kids."

"That's okay. I remember that day too. I'm still very thankful that Dixon has a real coffee shop." Carli stood on her tiptoes to watch Belinda pour the frothy milk into the cup. "Hold the whip, please."

"So, what is this about a 'no Christmas' drink?"

Carli didn't answer right away, pretending to dig in her wallet for money. "It's a long story, and I'm not sure I can explain it." Nor did she want to. Self-analysis made her irritable.

"I'll be here all afternoon and I'm all ears." Belinda counted out Carli's change and then made herself a glass of iced tea. She pulled up a stool across from Carli, the sound of chair legs scraping the cement floor bounced off the walls.

"Well?" Belinda stared at Carli calmly. Patiently.

Carli couldn't see any way out of this conversation. Would it be too rude to just get up and leave?

Chapter Fourteen

Monday, B & R Beanery, Early Afternoon

Belinda sat on a stool across the table and kept her eyes glued to Carli, waiting for an answer. They were the only ones in the coffee shop. Carli took her first sip of a French toast latte and could feel the tension seep out of her shoulders. No holiday music. Minimal decorations, simple but cheery. Thank goodness.

"Well? How is it?" Belinda watched her intently take another sip, like a chef awaiting the culinary judge's verdict on her latest creation.

A smile slowly spread over Carli's face as she stared off into the distance. "Cinnamon. Maybe a hint of vanilla? No, it's maple. That's it. Delicious."

"Glad you like it. Now tell me, why this avoidance of Christmas? I'm guessing it's not just directed at beverages."

Carli stared at her mug, savored another taste, and wondered how she could give excuses in a polite way without offending her friend, and just go home. But she forgot to ask for a to-go cup and she wasn't about to leave this savory drink behind.

"It's like any other day to me. The couple who raised me weren't big on celebration. All of the commercialization drives me crazy. I just don't get it."

Belinda studied her for a moment. Outside the engine of a pickup truck minus a muffler chugged past, the sound lingering in the air for several blocks.

"This is my favorite time of year, so I'm having a hard time relating to what you just said. Didn't you get presents as a kid from your guardians?"

"They were older, not used to having a young kid around. Our holidays were very low key. After the Fitzgeralds both passed, I never thought about exchanging gifts with anyone. That first Christmas on my own went by just like any other day, riding horses, mucking out the barn. I stayed so busy with my horse business, the holiday came and went and then it was a new year. The years kept ticking by and I stayed busy. Before I knew it, I had survived a decade without putting up a Christmas tree."

"You have a practical, nonchalant way about you which keeps your heart guarded. That isn't always a good thing, Carli."

"Right or wrong, it's the hand I've been dealt. Nothing I can do about it." Carli broke Belinda's intent gaze to stare into her almost empty mug. Thank goodness. A few more swallows and she could leave, but then again, a refill would be nice, and she'd remember to ask for a to-go cup this time. The conversation was causing her to dig deep, and she didn't like it.

"My family has always celebrated this time of year in a big way. Actually, going overboard you might say. We pick a different theme for decorations every year. My mom and I alternate hosting the family dinner, but we help each other decorate and cook. This year it's at my house and the theme is snowmen, which reminds me—" Belinda slid off the stool disappearing behind the counter and returned with a glistening, white cookie sporting a painted face and red frosting for a hat. "You should come look at our family room tree. The topper is a big snowman head, and I flocked the tree by myself. The kids made snowmen ornaments out of toilet paper rolls." She laughed. "Hmm, I can see by the look on your face you'd rather muck out the barn than have a look at our tree."

"I'm sorry but I don't have a crafty bone in my body, and I'm not even going to ask how you turn a toilet paper roll into a snowman. Honestly, I don't think I want to know." Carli admired the cookie before taking a bite. "How did you get this to sparkle like that?"

"Edible glitter."

Carli bit into the cookie. Flaky and buttery tasting, the fluffy icing added just the right amount of sweetness. "I taste almonds. That's a surprise."

"I'm thrilled you have such a discerning palate and can figure out the ingredients. You are now the official B&R taste tester." Belinda laughed and patted Carli on the back. "I usually don't share my creations, but for you I'd be happy to give you the recipe."

Although Carli would have liked to sway the conversation away from holiday talk, she asked about the decorations. Belinda explained. "We buy a plantable evergreen. I use the trimmed branches from previous year's trees, to decorate now. Just like my grandma and her grandma before her, because of our German ancestors. I kinda go crazy with it. The everlasting evergreen tree is a symbol of God's love. Russell is of Mexican heritage, so we have tamales on Christmas Eve. You should join us for Midnight Mass. Please? The holiday is no time to be alone."

"I think that's the day Buck and Lola will be back and they're expecting me for dinner. Thank you for the invite, but I should stick around ranch headquarters." Carli grimaced. The last swallow of her coffee was cold.

"Well, if you change your mind. You know you're always welcome, Carli. In all the frenzy, this time of year also brings a stillness to my heart. I reflect on the faces around the table and think about the ones who aren't here anymore. I really miss my grandmother and I'm sorry you never really knew yours. The holiday is what you make of it." Belinda walked behind the front counter to refill her tea. "So how about you? What's going on at the Wild Cow?"

Carli summed up the morning milking episode which had Belinda holding her sides with laughter, tears ran down her cheeks, and caused Carli to collapse into a fit of giggles. It was funny now and all so absurd.

"I wish I could have seen you." Belinda wiped her face with a napkin. "If you can't go to Mass, how about Christmas Day? Eat lunch with us."

Carli pushed her stool back. Although she had

no intention of going anywhere that day, she was glad to have an excuse. "Got an invite already but thank you."

"From who?" Belinda stood and followed her to the door. "Don't make me drag it out of you."

"I'm eating at the Rafter O Ranch. Nathan invited me."

Belinda gave her a sly grin and punched her arm. "That boy sure is easy on the eyes. Is this the beginning of something?"

"I think we're just friends. I can't figure out exactly what's going on. My heart is tugged elsewhere, though."

"Would you like a dozen snowmen faces to take back to the ranch?"

"No thanks. It's just me this week. Buck and Lola are visiting their niece and Lank went to his sister's." She hesitated for a second. "Make it half a dozen."

They both laughed. Carli followed Belinda back to the counter while she boxed up the cookies. She dug for her wallet.

"Put your money back. Cookies are on me. Seriously, Carli, I can't imagine you giving your heart to anybody, although I wish you would. You can be so guarded, and I say that as a friend. You're in Texas now. Our rule is too much information at all times. And obviously you've been holding back. So, spill."

"Nope. That's all you get for now. Gotta go. Enjoyed the coffee and chat." Carli turned just before she stepped outside. "Thanks for being my friend in this town, Belinda."

"Don't mention it." She placed the carry-out box

in Carli's hands and leaned closer to give her a hug. "If you need anything, just let me know. Merry Christmas, friend."

Carli suddenly remembered what she had meant to ask. "Oh, I almost forgot. You wouldn't happen to know anyone who owns a milk cow, would you?"

"I thought you knew already." Belinda looked at her like it was the strangest question ever. "Your neighbor, Crazy Vera. I'm almost certain it's her cow. I've got her number somewhere. You want it?"

"My neighbor? Where does she live?"

"Vera Allgood lives just across the east fence line from your North Pasture. I think you can see her house on the hill right at the cattle guard." Belinda handed her a neon yellow sticky note with a phone number neatly printed on it.

"Why do they call her Crazy Vera?"

"If I ever knew, I've forgotten now. I'll ask Mama tonight."

"How do you know so much about my ranch?"

Belinda's cheeks turned a rosy pink and she grinned. "I used to date a boy that grew up there. His father was the horse trainer several decades ago. Spent a lot of time at the Wild Cow, but then my Russell swept me off my feet and I lost interest in any other boy after that."

"You knew my grandparents then?"

"Yes. Quite well in fact. This was your grandmother's favorite time of the year. She was all about the sparkle and fuss, and the people too. You should have seen the ranch. Your Grandma Jean used to say, 'It takes a lot of effort to make headquarters look this garish.' It was over the top, but the community loved it. Jean kept Ward and Buck busy most of November. Lights everywhere. Red bows on every fence post. It was so beautiful. Even after Russell and I married, I helped Jean and Lola make cookies. We must have handed out hundreds of cookies every year."

"I've got groceries in the pickup, but I want to hear more about my grandparents one day."

"Sure, I'd like that. Good luck this week by yourself. And, Carli. They would be so proud of the young woman you've become and so happy that you're at the Wild Cow. Too bad they didn't live to see you come home."

Despite her best efforts, Carli climbed into her pickup truck with tears stinging the backs of her eyes. Is this really where she was meant to be? Home? How come every day that went by reminded her that she was the outsider?

Her mood lightened and she had to smile. "Why would anybody save their toilet paper rolls to make holiday decorations?" She giggled.

Chapter Fifteen

Christmas was her grandmother's favorite time of year, Belinda had told her at the coffee shop. "They'd be so proud of you...happy that you've come home to the Wild Cow." She tried to imagine the ranch headquarters as Belinda had described it with lights on every building and the barns. It must have been a beautiful sight. No wonder people drove from town. And her grandmother handing out cookies.

How could Carli be so opposed to the holiday? Such a Scrooge. She knew why. Because she had been robbed of those happy times with family. She had no family. She had been abandoned. By her own mother.

What a day it had been, her first day alone on the ranch, the only one to oversee the animals and do all the work. There's a crazy dairy cow in her front yard, and obviously the sheriff might be annoyed a little; he didn't want to be bothered. The morning was finally behind her, and she had managed to shop for groceries and drink a coffee. Her day was complete.

She enjoyed the sanctuary of her own space, away from people and all their talk about the holiday, and her grandparents. She was looking forward to a peaceful evening.

But she couldn't help being curious about them. Who had they been? What kind of people? They were her blood after all. She had come from them. Maybe she could learn more about herself if she knew more about them.

She had seen some rodeo photos on the walls and bedroom dresser. She had heard they were heavily involved in the rodeo circuit. Team ropers. Saw their smiling faces nearly leap out of the glossy photos, come to life.

But she wanted to know more.

With her groceries unloaded and put away, her mind drifted back to her grandparents. She remembered where she might look for answers. In the back bedroom closet, she hauled out boxes, pulled them to an open space, and sat down cross-legged. She leaned over and looked inside, anxious at what she might find and discover about the people who had lived here. Maybe there were a few family secrets.

One box contained ten or more photo albums. Carli smiled at the difference in technology over the years. Nowadays people kept photos on their phones. Physical albums were different. You could touch the pages as you flipped through the life events, the smiling faces.

Carli was impressed at how organized her

Grandma Jean had been with the albums. She had known some people back in Georgia who, when cleaning out their parents' and grandparents' homes, found loose photos scattered in a box, no rhyme or reason, no dates or names. Grandma Jean seemed to have cherished her family's life and took care in preserving the special events.

Carli lost track of time looking through the albums. There were a lot of photos of Grandma Jean and Grandpa Ward at rodeo events—always smiling, decked out in their rodeo outfits, racing around on their horses in the arena, standing next to their horses accepting trophies, ribbons, belt buckles. Hugging each other, even kissing on the cheek. Their love was reflected in their eyes and jumped off the page. A force to be reckoned with, Carli thought. And if she got this feeling from photos, what must they have been like in real life? Gosh, she wished she could have known them.

Most of the albums were 1960's-1970's style, plastic sheets pulled over the photos on the pages. Some covers had funky flower designs or bright colors. Some were of a Western motif—horses, cattle, cowboys.

In one box Carli found decidedly older albums, maybe from the 1940s. Longer, black or brown covers held together with some sort of tie—like a red or black shoestring. Four-inch square, black and white photos had been placed in little corner holders stuck on black pages. Were those people her great-grandparents?

She'd have to go down that era's memory lane some other time. Right now, she opened a box that held stacks of letters, bound with ribbons. Her curiosity got the better of her.

One was addressed to Miss Jean Jameson from Mr. Ward Kimball. It must've been before they were married. Ward had poured his heart out to Jean in letters. A lot of lovey-dovey devotion and shared dreams for their future in rodeos and running the Wild Cow Ranch. Carli opened a second letter but felt intrusive as she started to read about the blossoming love between them. Was it right of her to trespass as a spy into their personal life? She was kind of embarrassed.

She picked up a bundle of letters tied with a pink ribbon. Addressed to Michelle Jameson in California. Unopened. Returned to sender. Rubber stamped, "Addressee Unknown." This was her mother. She felt she had a right to open them.

"Dear Michelle, I'm not sure this letter will find you, but I had to try. We've been told this was your latest address. We're praying that you're safe and well. Whatever you might be thinking of us, whatever has been said in anger or tears, please know that we love you with all our hearts. Please forgive us for anything we may have done to cause you to leave your home.

"Michelle, you are our child, our baby girl, our only child. We have loved you since before you were born. We've prayed for you day and night. We will always love you. No matter what. All is forgiven. We hope you can forgive us. We never meant to hurt you. We're sure we made mistakes and wish we could change what was done in the

past. But we can't.
"And if you have your own baby girl now, we'd
love to see her, our granddaughter. We'd love to
see you. Please come home.
"Love always, Mama and Papa."

Tears were blinding Carli's eyes. Such heartache. Her poor grandparents. From their letters, Carli could tell they loved their daughter deeply. Did Michelle receive the letters and return them unopened? Or had she already moved on to another place? Carli's lawyer had told her that the grandparents tried to find Michelle with the help of a private detective but were not successful. Michelle was running and would never return to the Wild Cow Ranch.

But Carli had. And maybe if she knew more about her mother and grandparents, maybe that would help her to move forward. To know what kind of person she wanted to be. To make good choices with her life. Unlike her mother.

Right now, her stomach grumbled. And she was exhausted. Physically and emotionally. Tomorrow would be her second day of running the ranch on her own. She needed food and sleep to get ready for it. Reluctantly, she stood and ambled into the kitchen to find something for dinner.

An hour later, a nice shiraz wine, a chicken breast cooked slowly in butter and garlic, and a huge salad were the results of her work. It all smelled so good, and her stomach was ready to dig in. Carli had even made extra for easy lunches over the next few days. She pulled her chair up to the dining room table, struggling a bit as the legs gripped the plush rug. Heavy and solid, what was the story behind the furnishings in her grandparents' house?

One discovery in her grandmother's belongings was several sets of china placed in neat stacks and filling the bottom of the cabinet. She chose a heavy beige pottery with brands encircling the rim and the head of a Texas Longhorn in the middle. One of the dinner plates now held the chicken. She had selected a navy-blue cloth napkin and on that placed heavy, ornate silverware. Candles were a last-minute thought. "Dinner for one," she mumbled and smoothed the napkin in her lap. Glancing at the group of candles, she appreciated their warm glow and the shadows cast around the dining room. The wine glass was unique too. Delicate etched vines and leaves trailed around the rim. Sipping slowly, she savored the rich earthiness as it rolled to the back of her tongue.

Carli reached for her cell phone to find some music, and then decided against it. The house may seem quiet, but, as old buildings always do, it had sounds of its own. Creaks and thumps didn't bother her. Being alone had never troubled her. Admittedly, for the first time at the ranch she felt a calm. It felt right to be sitting in this dining room.

Maybe she should have invited Nathan. It would have been nice to have company and to share pride in her ability to take care of the ranch on her own. Problems faced and handled. "Go me." She smiled.

But then another part of her was afraid. Afraid to start something. Afraid of getting hurt because the sting from her previous boyfriend remained just under the surface and she still fought to keep it buried. Although she didn't feel the tug of Nathan like she did for Lank. Her ranch hand was never far from her thoughts. Nathan was becoming a good friend, and it would have been nice to have him over for dinner. But the face that kept hovering in her mind's eye was Lank's. She wondered what it would be like to have him in the kitchen helping her cook. Having him sitting across the table from her. He probably didn't even like chicken. Most Texas cowboys didn't.

She stabbed a piece of chicken and told herself to stop thinking of men. She didn't need a relationship right now, particularly a complication with a neighbor or an employee. What was she thinking?

Concentrating on every bite, she looked down the length of the dining room table and wondered about the people who might have filled those now empty chairs. The smiles. The laughter. The hugs. Her heart stung to think she had been left out. Pushing the sadness away, she began making a To-Do list in her mind as she ate. Instead of calling her neighbor Vera about the dairy cow, she decided to drive over in the morning and introduce herself. Something kept nagging at her brain, like when you pack for a trip and as you drive away you just know there's something you forgot. But nothing had been left undone, right? Everybody was fed and snug, ready for the night. She had hidden the box of Belinda's cookies out of sight, but right after eating dinner unhid them and ate one anyway for dessert.

After the dishes were done, she relished the simple pleasure of a long, hot shower, took the time to condition her hair, blew it dry, and with a full sigh, sank into the cotton mattress that was no telling how old. With covers pulled up to her chin, she closed her eyes and drew in a deep breath, feeling her muscles unwind. The sheets were cool, but the bed warmed up fast, her skin still hot from the shower.

Horses are fine. Dairy cow is fine. Doors are locked. This ranching business is a piece of cake. She sat bolt upright. "Cake! Cows need cake."

She forgot to feed the cows their supplemental winter pellets which was supposed to be done on Monday, Wednesday, and Friday. Now the entire feeding schedule was off for the week. Collapsing back into the mattress with a frustrated huff of air, she'd have to do it first thing in the morning. But no, she needed to get the dairy cow home first.

Buck would be back on Friday, so maybe he could feed Saturday instead although that was Christmas Eve. If she could make one round with the feeder tomorrow, then she could run it again on Thursday. Or maybe do half the ranch tomorrow and half the ranch on Wednesday, but those later pastures would then go without for two days.

"Oh, good grief, Carli. You are such an idiot!" She said aloud to the dark room.

Chapter Sixteen

Tuesday Morning, Day 2 Alone

After feeding the horses and breaking ice in their water trough, Carli was still mad at herself for forgetting to cake the herds yesterday. She couldn't decide how to fix the feeding schedule, so instead sat on the top fence rail watching her calf, Maverick. Solid black, the Angus bull munched on the food pellets. He glanced in her direction with adoring eyes; if cows could show love. She believed they could. His shaggy winter coat and the way the fluff of curls covered his forehead made her smile. In the early fall, he was started on a bottle, right after her first visit to the Wild Cow. And she saved him from a horrible mutilation of his boy-parts. Then, seemingly overnight, her sweet bottle calf turned into an almost four-hundred-pound bull.

Although Mav seemed content to wander around the corral, he was becoming a handful. He buried his head in the round bale of hay, tossing it all over the pen, and then plopped down in the clean piles instead of eating it. One morning he was standing inside the middle of the round feeder like a jailed prisoner. How he got in there, nobody could figure out.

One day he scratched his head against the water tub until he turned it over and broke off the spigot. Water shot out over the round pen turning it into a muddy quagmire of wet, wasted hay and manure. It took Buck and Lank most of one day to replumb and repair the leak.

"You behave today. I don't have time to clean up your messes." Since he was still young, she couldn't put him in the bull pasture. Buck told her the bigger bulls would try to fight him. He needed to grow some more so he could hold his own in a scrape. Until then, he remained near headquarters grazing a small triangle of grass and roaming between pens. He needed a bottle twice a day, but he sure liked nibbling at the feed the bigger cows got.

Jumping off the fence, Carli hurried to the feed truck, shaking her head in frustration. What an idiot. She could hardly believe she had forgotten to cake the cows on Monday. "You had one job," she muttered.

Toting a thermos of coffee, jug of water, and snacks, she was not going to be deterred from this task until it was finished. Deciding about the route, should she drive to the farthest pasture and work her way back towards headquarters, or just get busy? First, drive through every pasture and take a head count.

"Might as well get to it." She steered the truck into the nearest pasture.

The herds tended to stay close together during the winter months, grazing on whatever they could find and keeping a sharp ear out for the siren on the feed truck. In the first pasture she found them at the bottom of a long, shallow valley not far from a windmill. Some turned, heads erect, intently watching as she topped the hill. She steered off the road into the pasture to drive in their direction. Flipping a switch, the foghorn sounded in the early morning air, and they came running.

Picking a clean patch of flat, grassy pasture free from clumps of yucca, Carli honked her horn again waiting until the herd surrounded the truck. Her phone list noted seventy-five momma cows in this pasture, and that's three pounds of pellets per head. Turning on the automatic feeder and driving in a straight line, she counted the clanks as it dumped food pellets on the ground. "Seventy-five," she said aloud on the last one and turned the switch off. As the cows ate, she drove back by the line and counted. Everyone was present and accounted for.

The next two pastures were much the same. The herds were found easily, and they came running when they heard the horn. Counts were good. Heifers were in the next pasture, a group of sixty young ladies who had not become moms yet. Low birth weight bulls would be turned in with them this coming spring, and the cows would have their first calf the spring after that. Bull genetics was one part of cattle ranch work that fascinated Carli. A rancher could breed certain favorable characteristics into future herds. Buck said she could go to the auction with him and pick out the new bulls they'd need.

Her life was so very different from her previous job at a real estate office back in Atlanta, Georgia and horse shows on weekends, to sitting alone inside a feed truck on a cattle ranch she now owned. Still, so much to learn. After moving here, she thought a lot about the horse shows. Training horses and working with clients had been her passion, and she missed the competitions, although she didn't miss some of the cutthroat competitors. But she had a peace here that she'd never experienced before in her life. Maybe it really was God leading her to Texas, as Buck and Lola kept telling her.

Carli drove for a good twenty minutes through the heifer pasture looking for the cows. First, along the main county road and then turning off onto bumpy tire tracks divided with tufts of long dead wildflowers and grass. She followed the pasture roads that snaked through the brown grass leading to windmills. Sometimes she actually pinched herself. The grass for as far as she could see belonged to her. Joy and then a deep sadness overtook her when she thought about the people who had worked this land for generations. It was her responsibility now. And that was overwhelming. She pushed the worry from her mind and focused on the task at hand. Find the missing heifers.

She stopped twice to replace mineral block, but still no cows in sight. After one round, she turned back onto the caliche road to make another. She found no animals. Something was very wrong. There were some parts of the pasture that she could not drive over in the bulky feed truck. The section of land was divided by a shallow washout that ran full in the rainy season.

Carli decided to go back and saddle Beau. While at ranch headquarters she called Sheriff Anderson on his cell. This was definitely life or death. If they lost their replacement heifers, it would be the end of the Wild Cow Ranch. They wouldn't survive the next couple of years without healthy calves to sell.

"Carli?" Sheriff Anderson answered with a growl.

"This is major, Sheriff. Cattle rustling is a matter of life or death."

"What's wrong?"

"Rustlers! That's what's wrong. I'm missing a whole herd of heifers."

"Okay, I'm on my way."

Driving back to headquarters, and in the saddle within minutes. The heifers were just one pasture over, so she loped to the gate with newfound determination. Maybe they were huddled in a creek bottom, hidden within a clump of wild plum bushes. Or worse, maybe they had gotten out. She decided to look for a break in the fence, so she kept close to the barbed wire with Beau lightly reined in at a steady pace.

From a distance, she saw what looked like a gap in the fence, and gigged Beau towards the twisted barbed wire. An old wooden fence post was broken off at the ground, and loose strands of wire lay on the grass. The top wire had snapped.

Steering Beau carefully through the gap, just like in her horsemanship classes from the past, she noted the churned-up ground. It appeared the heifers were all together and had been on the move. She tried to determine their path for a good mile, and then came to another fence. It too was pushed over and mangled. Looked like the entire bunch of cows had hit it at once. Hopefully, none were injured.

Behind her, she heard the crunch of vehicle tires. The sheriff's cruiser pulled off the ranch road onto the grass, heading in her direction. She loped Beau over to meet him.

"I inspected the gate into this pasture and saw no vehicle or trailer tires. We need to report this to a marshal with the Panhandle Cattle Raisers Organization."

Carli felt silly. She had forgotten about her panicked call to the sheriff.

"I think I found the place. The fence wires are broken over there."

"That's Crazy Vera Allgood's place. She's no cattle rustler." Sheriff Anderson stood straight with hands on hips, his shined boots dusty from walking across the dry pasture. His face changed to a deeper shade of red. "Did you call Dispatch first?"

"No, sir." This could have turned out a whole lot worse than it did. What if she had come upon rustlers and ended up in the middle of a shootout? She started to tell the sheriff as much but held her tongue.

"Ms. Jameson."

This wasn't going to end well, she just knew. Carli took in a breath, waiting for whatever was coming next. She looked at him, hoping he'd make this quick because she needed to ride through that gap and find her cows.

"I have an entire county to run, and I know you're here alone this week. But I say this with all seriousness, call Dispatch first." Sheriff Anderson tipped his Stetson back on his head and looked at her with steely dark blue eyes. "Do NOT call my private cell number again. Now follow the hoofprints. You'll run upon them at some point." His voice boomed with the "do not".

Carli already figured out that she had a trail to follow, so talking to her like a child didn't make the situation any better. The sheriff walked with purpose back to his cruiser and drove away without a wave. Back tires peeled out as they left the grass for the caliche road, sending a shower of rocks and sand behind the wheels.

Steering Beau carefully through the gap again, she studied the ground. As she topped the next rise, she saw the heifers standing in a huddle. All heads turned in her direction, reminding Carli of a group of naughty kids on the playground caught in a mischievous act by their teacher. At the top of the next hill, a beat-up truck slowly chugged her way, its loud engine echoed through the valley in stereo sound. Beau's ears pricked at the noise. The problem was that her cows were no longer on Wild Cow Ranch land, and if she was a betting kind of girl, she figured they were at Crazy Vera's place.

Chapter Seventeen

Tuesday, Mid-Morning, Vera Allgood's Place

"Hello, I'm Carli Jameson." She halted her horse next to a faded green pickup truck and bent over the saddle horn to look inside. Sprawled on the passenger side, or more like hogging the entire seat, was a liver and tan-colored bloodhound, his head twice the size of his owner's, but with a friendlier expression. Tail a'wagging and neck stretched towards the window. The woman shoved him back. "Move, Snot, you ole mangy hound.

"Are those your cows? You're trespassin'." She scowled at Carli.

"Yes, ma'am. I apologize, but there seems to be a gap in the fence, and these are my heifers. Are you Vera Allgood?"

"That's my name, don't wear it out."

"I guess we're neighbors. It's good to meet you." Carli smiled at the woman and couldn't help but stare at her greasy, wide-brimmed hat. A faded yellow wild rag, edged with lariats and longhorns, wrapped around her throat. "You have something of mine and I think I have something that belongs to you." Carli giggled at her own joke, but the leathery-skinned neighbor didn't crack a smile.

"Oh, yeah?"

"You wouldn't be missing a dairy cow by any chance?"

"You have my Honey Bun? I've been lookin' all over for her. In Texas we call that rustlin' and it's a hangin' offense, missy, in case you didn't know." Vera pushed back the floppy hat and her eyes narrowed into two mean slits that pierced right through Carli's bravado.

"She just appeared in my yard yesterday," Carli explained. "I had planned to bring her back today, if I can get her in my trailer, that is."

A little bit of the mad vanished from Vera's face and her lips turned up in a half-smile. "Good luck with that, girlie."

"So how should we go about this?"

With an exasperated sigh, Vera instructed. "Call Buck and tell him to bring his horse. We'll need some help. There's nothin' more fidgety snicket than a heifer in a tizzy when you're tryin' to put her somewhere she just don't want to go. It's like herdin' cats."

"Buck and Lank are both gone. I'm taking care of things this week."

"Lord, help us. You're Ward and Jean's granddaughter. That big city gal? Heard you was in town. You look just like your momma."

If Carli had a nickel for every time somebody pointed out who she was, she'd be able to buy a lifetime of lattes from the B & R. And Vera knew her mother. She'd ask about that one day. "Yes, ma'am, I'm from Georgia, but I do know how to ride a horse, if that's what you're worried about. I can call a neighbor at the Rafter O to help out."

Carli pulled her cell phone from the front pocket of her jacket. "Nathan. Hey. Bring your horse and come over to Vera Allgood's place. We need your help. As soon as you can." She disconnected. "He's on his way."

"Follow me then. I'll saddle up and hitch the trailer. The best plan I think is drive 'em in to my pens which are closest and then we can haul 'em back to your place. Let 'em out near the water, and then you'll have to hightail it over to the gap and repair the fence. With the three of us, we can get Honey Bun loaded and I'll bring her back home where she belongs."

Carli nodded. "Sounds like a good plan to me."

Vera made a wide U-turn through the pasture. Carli sat back a little in the saddle and gently cued Beau with one spur into a lope and followed Vera's flatbed truck.

The neighbor's pastureland looked much like the Wild Cow, with clumps of buffalo grass interrupted by an occasional yucca and some mesquite. The land rolled and stretched to the horizon. Carli kept her eye on the clump of trees that covered the top of the highest rise. That must be where Vera lived, the place visible from her pasture as Belinda had told her.

A narrow caliche road led to an arched metal entrance with the words, "The Rambling Riata." The sign on the gate read "Private Property" along with skull and crossbones. Bleached cow skulls hung from the posts here and there and dotted the ground. Another black and red placard hanging from the cattle guard depicted a picture of snarling Dobermans, announcing that trespassers wouldn't have time to dial 911.

A larger sign hung lopsided from the fence post and sported bold white hand-painted lettering that read: "WARNING. We don't aim to please—we aim to SHOOT."

Carli looked around wondering if anyone might have a shotgun trained on her, but she kept going.

As she followed Vera through the wire gate, she noticed a large pen full of goats. Carli waved Vera on and slid off Beau to shut the gate behind her.

Chickens crossed their path, pecking and scurrying for cover. "Wonder why they call her crazy?" Carli whispered aloud. Beau's ears darted back and forth as he shuffled to avoid the chickens.

Carli stopped Beau near the pickup truck.

Vera Allgood was a formidable woman, big-boned and tall with a long silver braid that reached to her waist and three earrings in one ear. A feather dangled from the other. "Come on, Snot." Vera opened the passenger door. The bloodhound lumbered out and settled in a shady spot under a screened porch. Carli loved his long ears and sad face and couldn't wait to pet him so she jumped off Beau and squatted in front of Snot. Holding her hand out for him to sniff, she scratched between his ears.

"That dog'll rip your hand off," Vera warned, but Carli saw her grin escape.

"What a handsome boy you are. You wouldn't

bite anyone." Snot's tail thumped against the wooden deck. She watched as Vera disappeared into the double-doors of a faded red barn. It was the size of a two-story building, rising to a peak in the center. On either side, one story metal roofs sloped down to cover the tin sides.

Carli looked around Vera's place. Not far from the barn a low stucco house featured a covered porch that stretched all the way across the front. More cow skulls hung from the posts and an oversized wooden rocking chair held center court between an assortment of benches and odd chairs. Native-inspired blankets and a few pillows covered the furniture. Carli felt like she'd just stepped back in time to the Wild West.

The one thing that Carli couldn't help but notice was a gravel path that led to a granite headstone in the middle of the yard surrounded by cactus, large rocks, and various planters. A gravel-covered mound made up most of the front yard. The side of the marker that faced the road was smooth. Carli couldn't see any words or symbols on the headstone.

Vera soon emerged astride the biggest dapple-gray horse Carli had ever seen. She couldn't help but stare, her mouth wide open. Vera was a sizable woman and on top of the draft horse, the pair made for an impressive sight. Carli wondered how Vera, not a young woman, had managed to climb up into the saddle. Maybe with a stepladder or mounting block?

Standing on the ground next to the horse, Carli's head barely reached his back.

Vera chuckled. "He's a beaut, ain't he? Part Percheron, part quarter horse. Despite his size, he makes a mighty fine cow horse."

"What's his name?"

"Pinto."

"Like a spotted Pinto pony?" Carli tried to hide her confusion without snickering.

"Nope. As in pinto beans. He likes to eat 'em. Little bugger destroyed my garden right after I got him. Ate up two whole rows before I could get him back into the corral." She leaned down and gave the horse a pat on his neck, her eyes sparkling with pride.

"I just have to ask. Is that a grave in your front yard?" Just as the question left Carli's lips the screen door opened and the largest pig she had ever seen walked out onto the front porch. "Is that a pig?"

"Jimmy Dean! You get back inside this minute." The pig made a sudden spin with a squeal and disappeared around the corner of the house. Vera turned to Carli. "That dang pig. Yes, that's the final restin' place of my Archie. God love him. Died after only five years of marriage." Vera's wide smile suddenly turned down into a frown and she swiped a tear from her cheek with a gloved hand. "He's my one and only soulmate."

"So, you never remarried then? I'm sad to hear about your husband."

"Lord no. I married again and buried that one too. Archie's just the only one that I really loved. The other was worthless. Only loved me for my looks and tried to steal my money."

Carli turned at the sound of tires crunching on gravel, thankful to be saved from that conversation. A shiny red truck pulling a shiny red livestock trailer parked right behind her and Beau. She waved at Nathan Olsen. The recognizable Rafter O brand, the letter "O" with a rooftop over it, stood out in white on the vehicle doors.

Nathan lifted a hand in greeting as he stepped from his truck and climbed out. "Good morning, ladies!"

"Thanks for coming on such late notice. The heifers broke through two fence lines and are now in Ms. Allgood's pasture. We could use some help getting them back home."

"The sooner, the better," Vera said. "I've got other chores to do, and it'll be lunchtime before ya know it. Archie likes to eat at straight up noon."

Nathan and Carli exchanged glances, and then he tipped his hat. "Happy to help, ma'am." He grinned at Carli. "Glad you called. My father was trying to find something to keep me busy. Even though we're all adults now, he hates it when his kids are idle. I was hiding out in the barn when you called." Nathan gave her a wide smile and winked. He hadn't shaved since she saw him last Saturday and his scruffy facial hair only made his handsome face and teeth look even more perfect. Carli felt her cheeks warm which was more embarrassing. When would she stop blushing?

"I'll be better when I get my Honey Bun back home. I rode all over the back forty last night lookin' for her. It was dang cold, too."

"Honey Bun, your milk cow? She's missing too?" Nathan asked as he opened the gate on his livestock trailer.

Carli glanced at him. Apparently, everyone knew who owned the milk cow at her house except for her. She never even thought of calling Nathan. "She spent the night at my place," Carli offered as she swung up into the saddle.

Nathan laughed. "Well, let's get everybody back where they belong then." He unloaded his horse.

"Get a move on," Vera called out as Nathan swung a leg over his saddle. "Them cows ain't gonna drive themselves."

Before long they were all loping across the pasture towards the Wild Cow Ranch heifers. Beau was still a little hesitant about those strange creatures called cows, but once he figured out what Carli wanted, he got busy.

The heifers were a real challenge. They knew which direction home was and didn't want to head towards Vera's place. It was a matter of riding back and forth behind the group, making the heifers stay together and moving in the same direction. Carli was proud of the way Beau seemed to understand what she wanted. He was getting better at cow work. With quick horses and teamwork, the trio soon had the entire bunch penned. Vera backed up her trailer and with Nathan's trailer they had the majority loaded. They'd have to make one more trip and come back for the rest. Carli and Nathan left their horses tied at the rail.

Vera opened the passenger door of her pickup and Snot came running without a call. She turned to look at Nathan. "No shenanigans on my watch! I see the way you pine for her, and don't think I don't know about you."

"Yes, ma'am. I mean no, ma'am." Nathan stuttered as he hurried to open the door and get into his truck.

Carli climbed in with Nathan. They both looked at each other and at the same time said, "She's crazy."

"And who is Archie?" Nathan started his truck and followed Vera out the entrance.

"Her dead husband, but he likes his lunch straight up noon." They both laughed again.

"How are things going over at the Wild Cow?"

Before she could answer, Nate punched a button and Brenda Lee's sultry voice explained the delights of rocking around the Christmas tree. "Turn that off."

"It's the Jolly Holly Channel," replied Nate. "They play Christmas music 24-hours a day right up until New Year's."

Carli could honestly say that she never got a sentimental feeling about anything around this time of year. She crossed her arms and remained silent, then grumbled, "I just don't like it, that's all."

"We need to have a serious conversation about your weird aversion towards Christmas."

"Nothing much to tell." Carli laughed. "And things are always happening at the ranch to keep my mind off the holiday. It's only been two days and I'm exhausted. Only three more days though until Buck and Lola get back. Surely nothing else can go wrong."

"We are in for a bit of weather on Thursday. Cold front moving in, but you can handle it."

"Thanks for your confidence. Sometimes I wonder what I'm doing here, and then other days it makes perfect sense that I own a cattle ranch in the Texas Panhandle." Carli looked out her window as they bounced over the cattle guard into the Wild Cow Ranch. What a crazy life. And her feelings about this time of year were too complicated to explain. She'd keep avoiding that conversation with Nathan for as long as possible.

Chapter Eighteen

Tuesday Evening

Getting her heifers back was a huge relief. Her heart calmed and the stress of the morning evaporated as she and Nathan left Vera Allgood's place with the last load. Vera followed behind. After they unloaded her trailer at the Wild Cow, she could drive on to ranch headquarters and pick up her milk cow, Honey Bun.

"I can't believe they tore through two strands of barbed wire fence, ran across two pastures, and then into Vera's place."

"Yeah, heifers are like that." Nathan's fingers scratched his whiskers. "Something spooked them. You'll probably never know what it was."

"Why is she called Crazy Vera?"

Nate laughed. "She is an intense personality. It took me a minute to remember her last name earlier. They say she ran off her second husband because he stayed drunk and never worked. She decided she was capable of running the place by herself. They always said she loved her animals more than him anyway."

"She just told me they both died, and yes, she does seem to have a soft spot for all of her critters. I just saw a pig come out of her house."

"Mom loves her goat's milk soap, caramel candies, and cheeses. Vera always has a booth at the craft fair. But she won't sell to you if you haggle over the price or if she doesn't like you. I guess that's where the 'crazy' comes from."

"She said she knew my mother. I'll have to talk to her about that one day." Carli wondered just how many people around Dixon remembered her mother. She'd like to talk to every one of them. Did they know her father? Maybe someone knew why Michelle ran away and hated the Wild Cow Ranch so much.

"And that horse of hers can sure herd cows, despite his size."

"Pinto. Yeah, he's impressive."

"Pinto? Like a Pinto pony?"

Carli laughed at the look on Nathan's face. "No, as in pinto beans. He likes them."

Nathan pulled off the road and parked near the windmill in the east pasture to unload the heifers. Vera drove her rig around them towards Wild Cow Ranch headquarters. It only took a minute to unlatch the trailer gate and get out of the way. The cows tumbled out of the trailer like a torrential stream, some backwards and some running full tilt frontwards while others backed up and refused to budge. It was a mass of red Angus hair and legs, wild eyes, all moving in a panic.

Carli had a paper and pen ready to make tick marks, but the heifers were too bunched up and excited. "I'll bring the feed truck tomorrow and get a count, but I think we have everybody."

"I'll help you fix the fence as soon as we get Vera's milk cow loaded into her trailer."

"Thanks, Nathan. You're a lifesaver. The sheriff's not too happy with me."

"Why's that?"

"I found his private cell phone number tacked to the bulletin board in the cookhouse. He said to only call for life or death matters. I'm to call Thelma at Dispatch first."

Nathan snapped his head around. "You called him about missing heifers?"

"I thought they had been rustled. I didn't know they'd broken through the fence. I guess I panicked a little and his number was at the top. I called him about the milk cow too."

"Oh, no." Nathan closed his eyes and shook his head. "That's not good."

Carli titled her chin and crossed her arms over her chest. "I am not going to call Buck or Lank. I want to show them that I can be responsible for my own ranch. What can go wrong in a short week? This is so stupid."

"Stop pouting and acting like a victim. A lot can go wrong on a cattle ranch. You have no idea. When you mix horses and cows and people, and then add weather to the mix, it's a combination for disaster. But we're used to it. People out here are tough and take it on the chin without a second thought. We just do what needs doing and go on to the next thing."

"I noticed that. No one gets riled up about anything around here." Carli couldn't help but feel like the whole universe was against her, and more importantly, Sheriff Anderson.

"You've just got to cowgirl up. How would getting upset solve anything?"

It was a few seconds before Carli answered. "I guess it doesn't, but never underestimate the power of a hissy fit."

Nathan laughed. "I can't imagine you throwing a fit of any kind. You always seem so calm."

"That's not what's going on inside. Believe me."

They pulled into Wild Cow Ranch headquarters. Nathan stopped between the saddle house and the shop. Vera had plenty of room to turn around and back up to the corral gate.

"And for your information, I am not pouting." Carli jumped out of his truck and slammed the door. The nerve of him. She heard Nathan's laughter follow her across the compound.

"Do you have any sweet cow cake handy?" asked Vera as Carli and Nathan got closer.

"Sure. In the saddle house. I'll go get it." Carli needed to walk away from Nathan for a minute anyway.

When she returned, Vera took the bucket and placed it under Honey Bun's nose. "Looky here what I have for you, sweet thing." The cow shoved her head into the bucket and raised up munching, looking around.

Nathan held his hands out as he slowly walked towards Vera's cow.

"Should we stand back?" asked Carli. So far, Honey Bun had seemed gentle, but animals could be unpredictable when crowded.

"Oh, she's as gentle as a kitten. She just doesn't care one way or another." Vera suddenly took the bucket from Honey Bun and placed it in the trailer. The cow looked at Vera, then at the trailer, and then looked back. "You know what we want. Get a move on now."

The three of them crowded closer around the cow, driving her towards the trailer.

"Let's go home," said Vera, delightful energy in her voice.

Honey Bun kept chewing on the cow cake. She took one step forward. Then another. And then ambled across the pen to the water trough.

"Come on, girl."

"I've got a hotshot in my truck. I'll get it." Nathan placed one foot on the fence rail and easily climbed over in one fluid motion.

"You'll do no such thing! If you touch any of my animals with that hotshot, I'll be using it on you next, Cowboy."

Carli had no doubt that she would too. Nathan came to a halt and spun around. "No offense, ma'am."

They stood silent and watched Honey Bun drink her fill. Carli couldn't stand much more. Were they going to have to stand here all day waiting for the cow to make up her mind?

"Just get behind her and keep talking nice. Make your voice sound real friendly. She can tell when you're faking." Vera shot Nathan a squinty glance which would have scared most men.

Nathan looked at Vera like she had grown two heads and a tail, but he kept his opinion to himself.

Carli clamped her lips together tight to stop the

giggle that was bubbling up from her throat. She almost choked. "Pretty girl, let's go."

"This way, Honey Bun. Walk this way." Nathan even joined in, rolling his eyes as he spoke softly to the cow. Carli stifled another giggle.

Finally Honey Bun decided she'd get on the trailer in her own time and finish the cake.

Vera slammed the trailer gate shut with a loud clank. "I'll get that bucket back to you soon. Thanks for your help." As she hurried around to the driver's side, she came to a halt. "What's that?"

She pointed across the corral to Maverick. He had his head stretched over the fence rails, nose wiggling in the air, ears twitching.

"That's my bottle calf. Well, he's a little stunted because his momma died, and then I convinced Buck to keep him a bull. He's a handful." Carli couldn't help but smile when she looked at him.

"He's a bull, ya say?" Vera ambled over the fence rail, surprisingly limber and light on her feet for her age.

"Yes, ma'am. All the working parts are still intact." Carli didn't dare get in the pen with Maverick. He thought of her as his food source and had gotten so strong, he usually nudged her off balance.

Vera went up and over the next fence and walked right up to the little bull calf. She leaned against his side and scratched between his ears. Maverick leaned in closer. "How much you want for him?"

"He's not for sale," Carli answered without a second thought.

"I need me a bull for my herd, and he'd do just fine." Vera bent closer and whispered in his ear.

"I don't think I can let him go." Carli frowned.

Maverick belonged with her. They were buddies. Mavericks, all alone in the world, orphaned.

Vera turned and directed her gaze straight to Carli. "I don't have any other bulls. He wouldn't get beat up. That's why you keep him in here, isn't it? Wouldn't he be much happier in a pasture?"

That sealed the deal for Carli, besides it was hard to argue with Crazy Vera. "How does fifty bucks sound?"

"That's way too cheap." Vera shook her head in disagreement.

"He's not registered," Nathan offered.

"Doesn't matter. I'll give you $200. Deal?" She stuck out her hand and Carli shook it. "Let's load him up then and I'll be on my way."

Nathan walked across the pen and opened Maverick's gate. Giving him a wide berth, Nathan walked around the outside of the pen to get behind him and then raised his hands. "Get on now, Mav."

The bull hurried through the opening and ran straight to Carli. Her heart tugged as she scratched him behind the ear. Vera coaxed Honey Bun up to the front of the trailer, shut the gate inside, and they loaded Maverick into the back.

Vera counted out cash and placed it in Carli's hand, but Carli couldn't say thanks or goodbye. Instead, she choked back the tears and swallowed the lump in her throat as Vera waved one last time and drove away with Maverick.

That bottle calf had been the first responsibility she felt she could take on when she came to the Wild Cow. Maverick had needed her, and she had needed him. They were both alone, lost. Good grief, she was acting ridiculous. He wasn't good for anything. She'd have to feed him the rest of the winter and spring until he was big enough to be turned out with the other cows, and then he'd have to be isolated from the main herd during breeding season.

"Don't be sad." Nathan slung an arm around Carli's shoulders. "Maverick is going to paradise. Vera will treat him like a king and then some."

"I guess you're right."

"Now, let's load up the fencing material and go fix that hole before the heifers find it again."

Despite her resolve to not be emotional, she paused to wipe a tear from her cheek with the back of a gloved hand before she followed Nathan to the barn.

"Are you hungry?" he asked as he led his horse to the livestock trailer.

"Not really."

Nathan removed the saddle and bridle, led his horse into the trailer, and filled the holder with fresh hay. Stowing his gear, he turned to Carli. "I'm going to help repair your fence. Where does Buck keep the fencing material? We're taking your truck."

Carli remembered seeing posts and barbed wire in one of the sheds, so she parked in front and watched Nathan as he loaded what they'd need.

Despite the fact that her stomach growled because it had been a long time since breakfast, the only thing Carli could think about was she hoped Nathan didn't adjust the radio station when he got back in her truck.

No such luck. Jolly holiday tunes blared in her ears while Nathan sang along. She was afraid to complain because that would only lead to more questions from him, she'd have to analyze her childhood, and then she'd lie awake all night reliving the conversation. A few more days and Christmas would be over. She was beginning to doubt if she'd make it.

Chapter Nineteen

Carli squinted her eyes as a gush of shampoo trickled across her cheek. Suddenly, the bathroom lights faded and blinked out. She stepped under the water stream to rinse, which soon turned into a dribble and then stopped.

"Oh, great." She felt for the towel and wiped some of the unrinsed shampoo from her hair. Yuck. Well, that's what hats were for. The sun was not yet over the horizon, so the bathroom was midnight black. Carli couldn't even see her hand in front of her face.

"Ow," she hollered as her bare foot met a boot heel lying sideways where she had taken them off the night before. Now if she could find her phone. She had planned to get an early start on busting ice in the water troughs this morning, and then work on her family genealogy in the afternoon. So much for that schedule.

She wrapped the towel around her and felt along the sink cabinet to the door frame. Keeping her left hand flat on the wall and her right arm stretched out in front, she turned down the hall and headed towards the spare bedroom. Her phone should be on the nightstand in her bedroom, connected to the charger. Or was it still on the kitchen counter? Buck had called last night to check in and she told him again that she was fine. She hadn't heard a word from her other employee, Lank, in four days.

She found it in the kitchen. By the light of her cell phone, she started to grind the coffee beans, but no electricity meant no coffee. With a heavy sigh, she went back to the bedroom to dress. Her first instinct was to call Sheriff Anderson, but now she knew better. He would be the last person to call. She needed to find an electric bill with the phone number to report outages. Find an electric bill without any electricity, great.

The ranch files were stored in the back room of her grandparents' house, which she wanted to make into an office. Lola had been doing the books and keeping the bills paid as a favor to Ward since Jean passed, but she now politely insisted that Carli take it over. Lola wanted to get back to cooking, canning, and gardening, which worked great for everybody. With Carli's experience as the office manager for a real estate broker in Atlanta, she eagerly agreed. It would give her a chance to really learn the business side of cattle ranching. She needed to figure out a filing system though. Carli pointed her cell phone flashlight around the room.

Boxes with ranch records were stacked against one wall, still where the guys had put them a month ago. Polished wood floors, bookcases that covered two walls with framed buckles, and award plaques in the others. Two overstuffed chairs were arranged around the small wood-burning stove. She imagined her grandparents sitting in this room every evening. And now in the semi-darkness, it seemed even more filled with their presence. She shook away the image. Maybe she could find the most recent power bill in a pile somewhere.

However, first order of business was her growling stomach. Carli remembered seeing a metal pot in the pantry and a bag of ground coffee in the freezer. She gave up on her search for the paperwork and headed to the kitchen instead. Since the stovetop was propane, she could make camp coffee. Better than nothing. Bacon and eggs fried to perfection in the cast iron skillet sounded good too. While the bacon sizzled, she searched through the cabinets and found a few candles.

With her stomach happy, she held a mug in one hand and a candle in the other and returned to the back room. In one corner, the wood-burning stove sat cold and empty as did the fireplace in the living room. The wood was stacked outside, covered in a dusting of snow no doubt. Why hadn't she thought to carry some in yesterday? She really needed to keep her mind on life on a cattle ranch in the middle of nowhere. Would she ever get the hang of it?

After a few more minutes of digging in a box labeled with dates from last year, finally success. "Found it!" she said aloud, peering at the minuscule emergency number on the back of the bill in the candlelight, and tried to dial. After she left her information on the voicemail, the sun was peeking over the horizon just enough to cast a faded glow on the windows. She might as well find her coat and get going on busting ice and feeding Beau some grain.

Her mind drifted to little Maverick. In a way it was a relief to not have to fix him a bottle twice a day, but then he was the one thing she had bonded with when she first came to this strange place. He had been all her responsibility and she liked that feeling. She wasn't sure if the baby bull had felt the same way about her, but she sure did miss him.

So far this week she had chased heifers and dealt with Crazy Vera, so now she needed to run the feed truck through several pastures. Or did she? She was supposed to feed every other day. The week was blending into a blur of days and nights, and she had lost track of what day it was. She had managed to feed a few head before discovering the missing heifers and she could finish caking tomorrow. Buck told her the crucial time to give supplemental feed was just before a big snow. He would have every-thing back on track next week. Hopefully, this afternoon she'd be able to get out her laptop and do some research on her birth father's side of the family.

Carli stepped out of the house, her breath hang-ing in the air. A light fog clung to the treetops. The rays of the sun were splintered by the gray overcast sky. Pulling on her work gloves, she trudged across the compound to the feed truck and cranked it up. Once inside, she wished she had brought a thermos of coffee just to keep her insides warm. The heater took forever to take the chill off the cab.

She drove through the first pasture, surveying

the rolling hills until she saw the herd, and then turned through the pasture towards them honking the horn. They froze and watched for a few minutes, and then moved towards her, some at a run. That's when the bawling started. She followed through the same process until all the pastures were done, and then realized she had forgotten the notebook with the cattle counts. She'd have to get an accurate count on Friday when she caked the pastures again. So much to remember. After this week, she really should consider firing herself. Thank goodness the Wild Cow Ranch came with competent help in the form of Buck and Lank. She was happy to be pulling into headquarters again.

Discovering no strange critters and no busted fences, the morning went well. That was the good part, but by mid-afternoon Carli stood in the entry hall of her house shivering. No electricity. Still no heat.

"I need a real coffee," she said out loud to the empty house, her breath hanging in the air. She grabbed her wallet and pickup truck keys. Thank goodness Dixon was not too remote to be without a coffee shop. She could have never survived otherwise.

Chapter Twenty

Lank Torres sat at his sister's kitchen table, digging into buttery pancakes, soggy with maple syrup. She added two more to his stack. Kelly cooked them just like his mom used to. Fried crispy on the edges from a blazing-hot cast iron skillet, but tall and fluffy inside.

"Only three pieces left. Eat this too." She placed bacon on his plate. "I need to finish up some Christmas shopping today. Would you and the boys like to go with me?"

His brother-in-law Matt had already left for work, and Lank had patiently agreed to doing whatever his sister had wanted. They spent most of yesterday afternoon at the mall already, plus a movie his nephews had picked. They had played countless hours of video games. Lank had more than done his contribution to family time and he really missed his quiet trailer. Sometimes he couldn't breathe here surrounded by traffic and people. There hadn't been a moment of silence except when he was asleep. And he missed his horses.

No less than one hundred times, he had wanted to call Carli to check on things. He just knew that she would call if she needed help with anything. She had to know he could be there in an hour. Surely, she wouldn't call Buck in Dallas before contacting him. Maybe he should call Buck. Just check in. Maybe he could take his nephews to the ranch this morning.

He worried that Carli would be upset if he showed up like that. The deal was she would watch over things for a week. If he popped in, would she resent him for checking on her? She was so hard to read, so guarded. He never knew where he stood or what she was thinking.

Noise like a herd of buffalo stomping down the stairs, both nephews descended on the breakfast table. How could two boys make that much racket?

"Hurry and eat, guys. We're going to the mall this morning."

Dejected looks and frowns covered both faces. "Malls are for girls," Zane the youngest, wise beyond his years, complained.

Lank laughed. Observant kid.

"Can **we** go to the zoo?" this from the oldest, Zachary, who Lank called Junior because he was the spitting image of his father. Curly black hair, dark complexion, and strong jaw. He was going to be a handsome man one day, plus he had his father's smarts too.

Lank perked up at that. "Fine idea, my man. Yes, we can." Lank sent a cautious glance to his big sister. "If it's okay with your mom."

"I suppose," replied Kelly as she poured milk into two glasses, and then refilled Lank's coffee mug.

That response resulted in the kitchen erupting into a frenzy of whoops and hollers and high fives.

"But eat your breakfast first," she said.

"Perfect timing, Sis. Load 'em up with carbs and sugar, and let Uncle Lank have them for the day."

She laughed. "Always here for you, little brother."

He smiled. It had been a good few days. The energy of his nephews helped to push the sadness away, even though it was almost Christmas.

With bellies full, Kelly helped the boys find long-sleeved waffle shirts to wear over their T-shirts. "You won't have to worry about keeping up with coats," she said. "They should be warm enough."

Lank thought it was brilliant. He didn't want to lug hats, gloves, and coats around, and risk losing them. Better to be safe than sorry had always been his sister's motto so he was glad she had thought ahead. They had to transfer a car seat for the youngest, and then she insisted on kisses and hugs, but finally everyone was buckled in. Kelly stood next to the driver's side window. "Boys, you mind Uncle Lank. Can you text me when you get there, and let me know what time you're leaving?"

"Sure. I will." Lank nodded his head. "We'll be fine."

"Okay, then. Have fun and I'll see you this afternoon." She took a step back and waved as Lank eased his truck into reverse and backed out of the driveway.

He couldn't help but smile at the unbridled joy that shone on the faces of his nephews. He felt just as happy, and then a bit of sadness clouded the moment. His mother loved these boys. One of the happiest days of her life had been when Kelly made her a grandma, and it stung to know that he would never be able to do the same. She'd never know his kids and they'd never know her, other than what he would tell them one day. His mother had left such a huge gap in their lives. And then his thoughts drifted back to Carli, as they always did.

Lank wanted a big family, although he wasn't getting any younger. He had no idea how Carli felt about kids. They hadn't even been on an official date yet. Mainly because he felt awkward asking the new ranch owner out. There was that, and the fact was sometimes he got tongue-tied when she was around. She was like a smoldering flame he couldn't extinguish yet refused to acknowledge what was happening inside of him.

"Are we there yet?" asked Zane.

"Do you see me pulling into the parking lot?"

"He always asks the stupidest questions," Junior grumbled.

"No question is stupid, and y'all can ask me anything, anytime," said Lank. "If you're ever in a bind, you can call me."

They nodded.

"The zoo exit," proclaimed Junior.

Lank took the exit and parked at the back of the half-full parking lot.

"Why are you parking way back here?"

"There's lots of spots closer."

Always super helpful, his nephews. And so, the day began with questions. "I don't like people parking too close to my truck. Walking won't hurt us."

They piled out of the vehicle and set out across the lot to the entrance. The Amarillo Wildlife Sanctuary sat on the far west edge of town on spacious acreage. Some of the animals had their own enclosures, like the monkeys, a reptile house, and the parakeet aviary, which they could walk through. On this mild winter day, the zoo wasn't crowded. The greeters at the entrance all wore red Santa hats with bright green jackets. Tinsel and blinking lights finished the festive feel.

"Snakes first," said Zane.

"No, the monkeys," argued Junior.

"Hold up," said Lank. "We have plenty of time to see everything. Let's not start the day with arguing. And do not run off by yourself."

"Yes, sir," replied Junior. He was always eager to please his uncle.

"Zane? Am I clear?" Lank asked.

The youngest nodded, but his eyes were darting here and there, energy pulsing from his little body. He wouldn't be able to stand still much longer.

"Monkeys are right here. Let's see them first and then we can go find the snakes."

They laughed at the antics of the monkeys as they swung from ropes and tires and hopped over the shallow stream that ran through their oversized cage. It was hard to leave them, they were so entertaining.

Lank stopped to look at a map, and then wandered towards the reptiles pausing once to admire a peacock that stood on the path, his tail feathers spread in full glory. The boys oohed and awed as they tried to name all the colors.

"I feel sorry for him," said Zane.

Lank and the boys stood on a raised deck looking into the bear habitat. A small brown bear pushed a big red ball around. It appeared he was alone. The little bear suddenly wandered over and walked closer to the thick glass. Zane dropped to his knees. "I bet he needs a friend."

"His name is Delbert, and he eats insects, berries, small mammals. His favorite thing is honey." Junior had been reading the plaques aloud all morning, regaling them with facts and information. Zane had ignored him, but Lank liked it. Saved him from having to read everything. Plus, he was proud of the boy's ability.

His phone beeped. He had forgotten to text Kelly. He answered her text, told her everything was going great, and that they were having a big time.

Despite the lack of flowers and lush leaves on the trees this time of year, the chirps and calls of the animals still made the grounds exciting. They saw everything there was to see, and then hopped on the slow-moving train which took them through the prairie dog town, bison habitat, and a small grassy enclosure with antelope.

"I'm hungry." Zane pouted a bit as they exited the train station.

"Me too," said Lank. "Let's see what we can find."

After consulting another map, they found the concession stand. Hot dogs, sodas, and crispy hot fries hit the spot.

"I want ice cream," said Zane after he had put away his lunch in record time.

"Sounds good to me," said Lank. "How about you, Junior?"

The choices were chocolate, vanilla, or strawberry, but all three ordered vanilla.

"Let's wander towards the monkeys again, and then we'll have to go home after you finish your ice cream." Lank led the way.

The boys laughed at the monkey antics. One squealed and jumped to the top of a tree limb, and others answered, their shrieks loud and shrill. Junior covered his ears. The animals went into a frenzy, jumping and leaping from branch to branch and rope swing.

"I need another ice cream," said Zane as he tapped Lank on the arm.

"I can barely hear you." Lank leaned down. "You can't have another one this close to dinner. You mom would skin me alive."

"But Delbert's eating mine," he said.

Chapter Twenty-One

"Zane! Good grief. You shouldn't be giving away food to kids you don't know."

Lank had been patient all morning, wandering around the zoo following his nephews, answering Zane's endless stream of questions, refereeing a few spats, and making sure Junior didn't get too far ahead. But he was about done and ready to go home now. He should find this kid's parents first. Maybe to apologize for Zane giving him food. What kid eats another kid's ice cream?

He turned. And froze. His heart dropped to his knees.

"He wants to come home with me," said Zane.

"Don't move. Stand still," Lank said between clenched teeth.

Delbert being a bear, not a boy.

Zane stood behind Lank, holding out the treat while the little brown bear licked the ice cream as though it was the most delicious thing in the world. His head was at the same level as Zane's shoulder. Lank glanced up to see an army of uniformed zoo workers marching their way like they meant business, one holding a long pole with a loop at the end.

The first thought Lank had was the workers might spook the bear and the bear in turn might hurt his nephew. There was no good ending to this situation that Lank could see. The group of men slowed, easing up cautiously. One man held his finger over his lips. Lank nodded. No sudden movement and no noise. The bear was still focused on the ice cream. Thank goodness Lank had let them get extra-large cones.

Junior was still watching the monkeys and had moved down the railing away from them. That was good.

At the exact same instance, Zane and the bear turned their heads and saw the men. The bear looked the other way to see an opening that led to the parking lot and freedom. In that exact moment, Lank said, "Oh no you don't."

The bear made a break for it and Lank lunged. With a full body tackle that would have made any coach proud, he rolled on his back pulling the bear with him. His arms full of thick hair and claws, snarls and squeals. It was a good thing the little bear's mother wasn't around since it sounded like Lank was hurting the cub. The zoo attendants rushed to them and looped the rope around Delbert's neck. Surprisingly Lank stood, unharmed. The bear tugged against the loop and lunged towards Lank again.

"He wants to play. His zookeeper wrestles with him all the time. Thanks for stopping him. You probably saved this bear's life."

"Wow! Did you see that?" Zane yelled at his

brother who stood frozen in place, a look of awe on his face.

"He's never gotten out of his enclosure before," one of the zoo attendants said.

"How did you know he would go for it?" asked another.

Lank shrugged. "I just knew. Maybe it's my experience around cows and horses. Never worked with bears before, but I could tell the minute the notion hit his brain. It's what I would have done if I was a bear."

After everyone checked on his health, Lank assured them he would be glad to sign a waiver. No harm and no lawsuits. It took another hour to sort it all out. Zane insisted on going with Delbert back to his enclosure.

Finally loaded with complimentary sodas, caps, and a stuffed bear for Zane, they were back in the truck and headed for home. Lank's first thought was he wished he could call Carli. She had become the one whom he most wanted to talk to. He had spent many a night in his trailer imagining their conversations, walking to the window to see if her lights were out. Trying to get up the nerve to just walk across the compound and knock on her door. But this time more than ever he wanted to tell her about his day and the time he wrestled with a bear at the zoo.

He cleared his throat. "Guys, we might want to keep this between us. Okay? No need to upset your mother."

Lank's comment was met with silence from his traveling companions.

"What'd ya say?"

"I guess so," murmured Junior.

Zane never answered. That couldn't be good.

He had forgotten to text Kelly again, and, since he was driving, he couldn't let her know that they were headed back.

Lank pulled into his sister's driveway, still uneasy about how to break the news. Maybe he could distract his nephews.

"How about playing that board game you guys wanted to play last night? Go get it set up and I'll be there in a minute."

They spilled out of the truck and beat Lank to the door, but he heard their feet rushing up the stairs. So far, so good.

"How was the zoo?" asked Kelly.

"It was great," answered Lank. He hung his cowboy hat on a hook in the entry hall and moseyed into the kitchen to find something to drink. He hid any further discussion behind the soda that he turned up and swallowed.

And then he heard feet again pounding down the stairs.

Zane dashed into the kitchen. "Uncle Lank wrestled a bear."

"It was awesome," said Junior appearing from behind.

Kelly's face went white and then she turned a glare to her little brother. "A bear?"

About that time Matt walked into the back door. "What's up, guys? What's for dinner?"

"A bear. Running loose at the zoo today." Kelly's hand shook as she sat down at the table.

"All right!" said Matt. "That's awesome."

And with that the boys exploded, both talking at once and trying to be the one to tell the story first.

Lank eased into a chair at the table, giving his sister a shrug and a look of apology. She gave him a half-smile.

"Who wants pizza?" she finally asked.

What a day. Lank reached for his cell phone and almost dialed Carli.

Almost.

With a sigh he slid it back into his jacket pocket.

Chapter Twenty-Two

Carli drove through the little town of Dixon, just another slow-paced, shabby little Texas town that newer generations couldn't leave behind fast enough. But this place was beginning to mean a lot to her.

In between the odd businesses with first name logos, other buildings stood empty, dust filled. In a few more minutes the familiar bell tinkled over the door of B & R Beanery & Buns as Carli walked in.

"Give me something hot with two shots of go-juice," Carli called out to the messy blonde bun just showing over the top of the espresso equipment. Her friend Belinda peeked around with a wide smile.

"Carli! Second time in one week? It's good to see you again. I'm going crazy around here. This cold has got everybody digging in. You'd think they'd want a coffee, but it's been a really slow day."

"Wish you could come out to the Wild Cow and help me. It's been anything but slow. And this morning I have no heat. It's freezing in my place."

Carli draped her coat over a chair back and slid onto a bar stool at the front counter, watching Belinda make her order. What the flavors would be was a mystery, but certain to be delicious.

"Try this on for size. It's got a kick to it." Belinda pushed a steaming mug towards Carli.

She moved her face closer and inhaled. "Chocolate. Maybe a hint of cinnamon." She sipped carefully.

"White chocolate latte with a little bit of vanilla and almond, and a double shot of espresso, just for you."

"This is gonna warm me up and improve my mood considerably." Carli dug in her purse and laid the money on the table. "Thank you."

After two soul-satisfying sips, Carli expelled her troubles of the past few days to her friend who sat on a stool beside her. Belinda feigned a sympathetic face sprinkled with "You poor dear", but couldn't hold in her laughter. "I'm glad you finally met Vera and got Honey Bun back home. Interesting that you spent a day with Nathan, too. Maybe there's hope for you being part of a couple before too long."

"I need to get back to headquarters and call the electric company again to figure out what the holdup is." Carli hopped off the stool, ignoring the "couple" comment, and pulled her coat on.

"Oh, you don't call the number on the back of your bill. You call Lester."

"Who's Lester?"

"I don't know his last name, but everybody knows Lester. He's the guy who gets the power back on in this county. I'm sure I have his number." Belinda darted behind the counter and Carli followed. Rifling through a drawer full of pens, scraps of paper, twist ties, plastic spoons, and various other random items, she finally produced a white index card with the name LESTER and a phone number written in purple ink. "Found it."

Digging around in her tote, Carli found a pen and an old grocery store receipt to copy down the info. "Thanks, Belinda. See you again soon."

She hated to bring it up again, but thought she'd ask anyway. "Why is it so important I become part of a couple?" Carli looked over her mug to watch Belinda's reaction.

"Nathan is so perfect for you. Y'all would make beautiful babies, and I love being married. Everybody should be married."

"I'm not having kids," said Carli. "And Nathan is a good friend."

"You two hooking up would mean a ranching dynasty in the county, bringing two cattle operations together. That would put the little town of Dixon on the map for sure." Belinda laughed.

"Maybe Dixon doesn't want to be on the map and maybe I'm not ready for a serious relationship right now. I have my hands full just figuring out why I'm here. I've got a lot to learn about cows."

"You'll find the one. This is where you're supposed to be. The whole town believes it." An all-knowing smile covered her face.

Despite her efforts, Belinda had steered the conversation back to her love life. Carli gave up and decided to let the subject drop. How was it that everybody knew for certain where she belonged except for her?

"Thanks for the coffee. I need to contact this Lester guy and get my heat back on."

"See ya." Belinda answered. "If you can't get Lester, let me know. Maybe somebody has another number for him."

"Will do. Thanks."

Carli walked into a bone chilling living room and thought better about removing her canvas Carhartt®. She had doubts about this elusive Lester. How could one man repair the power grid for the ranch? It had been almost twelve hours and still no heat. This was ridiculous.

What was the main number for Sheriff Anderson's office?

"Sheriff's Office. This is Thelma. How can we help you?"

"This is Carli at the Wild Cow Ranch. And I've been without electricity all day."

"Hang on please. I'll patch you through to Sheriff Anderson."

"Thelma! No! Wait!" This could not end well. Carli listened to the ring tone and thought about hanging up, but she was certain Thelma would rat her out, plus she was freezing and couldn't imagine trying to sleep in a frigid house. She tapped her boot toe impatiently as the phone rang.

"You got the sheriff."

"I am so sorry—" she began.

"Carli? Somebody had better be bleeding," was the gruff reply.

"I called Thelma like you said and then she connected me to you. We haven't had power out here since around five this morning. I reported the outage."

"Who'd you report it to?"

"I called the number on my power bill and left a message."

"Did you call Lester?"

"Who is this Lester and why does he care about my electricity?"

"Call Lester."

The line went dead. "Thanks, Sheriff. Nice talking to you too," Carli uttered in frustration.

She dialed the number Belinda had given her but got a recording saying it had been disconnected. Maybe she wrote it down wrong.

Dang. She'd have to call Buck after all.

Minutes later, Buck explained. "He's the service technician for our part of the county. Lives in Dixon. He can track the lines and find out what happened, and then get a repair crew out there."

"Sorry to bother you, Buck. I really appreciate your help."

"You call anytime. And Carli, we're not coming home today as I thought. Lola wants to stay until Christmas Eve, Saturday. But we're leaving early."

"See you then," Carli hung up before Buck could hear her giggle. If he would have asked her, she could have told him when he was coming home. They sure were characters. But she really liked and appreciated them. How could this place ever survive without them?

After assuring Buck that she could light the corner stove by herself, and careful not to transpose phone numbers again like on her first try, if that's what she did, she left a message for Lester. Thirty minutes later she was still working on warming the house.

Hauling in firewood from out back which was stored under a carport, she stacked several logs by the fireplace in the living room and two smaller ones in the corner stove in the back den. Using old newspaper, she got the fireplace roaring. The stove was a little more difficult, but it soon glowed bright with orange flames. Carli sank into the easy chair next to the wood burning stove and propped her stocking feet on the ottoman. She had no idea what she wanted for dinner, but at least she could get her toes warm. Big sigh. Thursday and Friday. Two more days. There was nothing left that could possibly go wrong this week.

Checking the weather app on her phone, she saw it would get below freezing tonight. In the morning, she'd break ice, cake the cows, and that would leave most of the afternoon to work on her genealogy. And then Friday would be easy sailing. She hadn't ridden Beau all week. If the weather were mild, that's what she'd do Friday. Go for a little ride, check on everything, and then Buck would be back. In the meantime, she needed food and a blanket, because it seemed that she'd be sleeping in this chair by the fire tonight. It had been only a few short days ago when she was excited about this week alone on the Wild Cow. But now she had a sense of brooding. Fate hadn't been kind. "Dear Lord," she whispered to the shadows that seemed to close in on her. "Please help me get through the next two days. Amen."

Chapter Twenty-Three

About to snuggle into her chair under a few blankets and in front of the toasty fireplace, Carli was almost resigned to sleep where she was. Her bedroom was still chilly. She hadn't done much for dinner, just leftovers, something to fill her belly. And she'd had a rough day what with the power being off forever, and the sheriff hanging up on her. She just wanted to hide from the world.

But that was not to be. Insistent banging on her front door nearly catapulted her from her snug nest in the warm cocoon of a chair. "Who the heck could that be? Maybe Lester?"

"Carli! You in there? I need to talk to you. Now!"

That powerful voice could only belong to one person. Crazy Vera. Now what in the world did she want? Carli wasn't sure of the time, and it probably wasn't that late. It's just that her house was freezing, she was bundled up, cozy in front of the fireplace, so she was in no mood for visitors. But she knew she had to answer the door. If she didn't, maybe Vera would push it down.

When Carli opened the front door, she caught a glimpse of the night sky. It wasn't really dark but soon would be. To Carli it felt like midnight since she was exhausted from her day.

"Hello, Miss Vera. Is everything all right?"

"No, it ain't all right, missy." Vera pushed her way in past Carli to stop just inside the door. "You gotta come to my place right away. That bull of yours is pinin' away for you. Won't eat. Doesn't want me to touch him. You have to come over. Now."

"C'mon in, Miss Vera, out of that cold." Carli opened the door wider and stepped farther back into the dark entry hall.

"Well, it's freezin' in here too, girly. Is your power off?"

"Yes, it is. Been off all day. I can't seem to get through to the power company. I'll try again in the morning."

"Did you try Lester?"

"If one more person tells me about Lester, I'm going to scream. Can I get you anything to drink? Hot tea maybe?" She turned and walked back to the kitchen. Vera followed.

By the light of a lantern, she filled the tea kettle and lit the gas burner with a match. Anything warm to hold in her hands would do since her fingers felt frozen.

"I think he's related to me. Maybe he's the brother of one of my husbands. Or maybe he's the nephew of a good friend. I'm not sure. Can't remember. But I betcha I could call him, and he'd make sure you have heat tonight. Would ya want me to do that?"

"Oh, that'd be great, Miss Vera. But isn't it getting kind of late? He wouldn't be working now, would he?"

"If I asked him to come out or fix it from wherever they have those fancy computers, you can bet yer bottom dollar that he would do it for me. In a New York minute. Now if I did that for you, Carli girl, there's somethin' you've gotta do for me."

"What is it? I'll try my best," Carli said as she filled two mugs with steaming water.

Vera's eyes bugged out and Carli thought the woman's voice was about to bellow like a roaring lion, just because of her stature. Instead, it came out like a purring kitten. "Please. You've gotta come see what's wrong with Maverick. I took a shine to him the minute I laid eyes on him, but the bond just ain't there. Maybe it will be one day. But right now, I feel like he hates me for taking him away from you, his real momma. I can't take it anymore." Vera collapsed into a chair at the kitchen table. "All my other animals love me. You've gotta come over, Carli. Or none of us are gonna get any sleep tonight."

Carli dropped a tea bag into her mug and the one in front of Vera. This large, imposing figure wearing a dark, oilskin duster and Russian-type, furry hat looked like she was ready to battle the frigid Antarctica. Instead, she was a big, old softy with a broken heart because a newly bought bull wasn't eating out of her hand and giving her kisses the way her pig, goats, and dairy cow did. Carli smiled but didn't dare laugh.

"Actually, I was about to turn in, Miss Vera. I've had a really long day. I'll be glad to check on Maverick tomorrow. I'm sure he'll be okay tonight. Just tell him good night and get yourself some sleep. He's probably just figuring out his new surroundings and—"

Before Carli could finish, Vera interrupted with the force of a hurricane as she slammed the palm of her hand on the table. No more sweet little kitten. "Nobody will sleep tonight! That bull is bangin' into the sides of his pen and hollerin' like someone is tryin' to kill him. I'm afraid he'll bust out. Then what? I'm beggin' you. You've gotta come tonight!"

There was no winning this battle with Vera. Carli would have to go out into the cold night to check on a bull. "As soon as I finish this tea, I'll put some more warm clothes on and be with you in a second, Vera."

Again, the kitten was back. "Thank you kindly, Carli."

When Carli was ready and came outside, Vera had her truck engine running. "Hop in. It's warm. I'll bring you home later. That is if you want to come back to this freezin' place. You can always spend the night with me and share a room with Snot if you want. He seems to like you."

Carli got in the truck that smelled of wet dog and any number of other unpleasant aromas. "But you'll call Lester soon, won't you?"

"Sure, I will. I'll do it right now. Don't you worry."

Vera grabbed her cell phone and pressed Lester's number on speaker. A tired voice answered, "Hello."

"Lester, old friend. This is Vera Allgood. I need your help pronto."

She explained Carli's power outage, said they needed it fixed tonight, no ifs, ands, or buts.

Clicking the end call button, Vera smiled at Carli. "There ya have it. Lickity split. Lester said he can check it from the power company's computers. He might just need to flip a tiny switch. If he needs to send someone out, he'll do that too. But he's pretty sure your house will be warmin' up in no time."

"Really? That's amazing."

"Yep. It's as easy as that. Once you get used to this close-knit community, you'll see that we all help each other. You just gotta know who to call and don't burn any bridges. Folks want to help each other."

Vera parked her truck near the barn and jumped out. "Now let's see what you can do about makin' Maverick comfy in his new home."

Even though Carli was cold and would rather be in front of her fireplace, her heart warmed at seeing Maverick. Her bottle calf had turned into a powerful, black bull. He looked even bigger since the last time she'd seen him.

"Hey, boy. What's going on with you?" She leaned over the fence and stood on a rail. Stroking his head, she murmured sweetly. "Now listen, Mav, you gotta be nice to Miss Vera. She loves you and will take real good care of you."

He butted his head against the fence, not abruptly or mean, but like a kid listening to her, wanting to get close. He didn't realize he wasn't a lap dog.

"Miss Vera, I'd like us to make up a bottle for him. I know he's outgrown that, but it'll be like a treat. It might settle him. And I want you to feed it to him. You're his mom now."

The big woman had all the fixings in the barn to make up the powder and add water to a big baby bottle although she rarely had the need for it with her livestock.

"All right, give it me," Carli said. "I'll get him started, then hand it off to you."

"You think this'll work?"

"It's worth a try, isn't it? Otherwise, I'll have to think of a Plan B."

Carli reached through the slats with the big bottle and Maverick found the tip quickly. He acted ravenous although there were plenty of pellets in his bucket.

After a minute of his suckling, Carli asked Vera to change places with her and take over the bottle. Maverick didn't seem to bat an eye; he just wanted the yummy mixture.

Vera held the bottle in one massive hand while stroking his head with the other. She bestowed soothing words of endearment on him. "That's a good boy, Mav. I'm gonna take real good care of you. And I'll find some nice, pretty girlfriends for you too. Would you like that, fella?"

The bull gurgled and slobbered until he finished the whole bottle. Some of the mixture had soaked Vera's hand and part of her jacket, which he proceeded to lick clean. She kept petting his head.

After a bit he belched and went to the other side of his pen, seemingly contented.

"I think he's gonna be fine now, Vera. Why don't we all get some sleep? Will you run me home, please? I'm hoping Lester got the power on and my place is toasty again."

"Sure thing, Carli. Let's go. Maybe when I get back, Mav will be sleepin' and dreamin' about his future girlfriends."

Carli yawned. "I sure hope so."

They both got in Vera's truck and before they

reached Carli's house, Vera said, "Thanks a lot, Carli. I think it's gonna work with Maverick. I'll let you know."

As they pulled up, all the lights were on in Carli's house.

"Yay! Power! That means heat. Thanks, Miss Vera." Carli's heart jumped for joy at the sight. Home.

"You're welcome. It's all about bein' neighborly. You're gonna fit right in."

For once, Carli believed there was no other place she wanted to fit in. This was home.

Chapter Twenty-Four

Thursday Morning, Day 4 Alone

The cold north wind smacked Carli's cheeks like an icy hand as she stepped up into the back of the feeder truck. Balancing on a cinder block, she stretched her arms to open the nozzle to the overhead storage bin. Cow cake supplement tumbled into the feeder on the back of the truck. A quick run through the pastures this morning and then Buck would be back soon. Carli smiled as she remembered Buck had told her Wednesday. Lola said Saturday. Whenever they got back would not be soon enough.

As the sun rose higher in the sky the blinding white pasture stretched for as far as she could see. A dusting of snow had settled over the ranch the night before. Not a deep accumulation but just enough cover to be bothersome with temperatures low enough to leave a crusty top on the water tubs.

After driving the feed truck this week, she realized the cows liked to bed down in low spots out of the wind. Down the middle of the Wild Cow ran a dry creek bed which flowed with water during the first spring rains. The rest of the year it stayed dry and that's where Carli looked for the herds.

She stepped out of the truck at the first stop, waiting for the Angus cattle to trot up the hill to where she had parked. Her boots crunched on the crusty white ground and her breath made steam in the air as she grabbed the axe from the truck bed. In a few minutes she had broken a hole in the ice and the herd gathered to watch her cautiously. Some crowded around the feed truck, sniffing every part of it. Back in the truck she turned on the feeder, got an accurate count, and hurried to the next pasture.

The morning went by fast. The cows were all together and came running as soon as they heard the horn. It wasn't until the very last pasture that things went awry.

The count was wrong. She steered into a doughnut and pulled back around to get another count. Still one missing.

Driving slow along the other side of the line as the herd munched on cow cake, she counted in a low whisper, sticking up fingers as each cow passed her field of vision in the window.

Minus one. Dang it.

"Now what?" she asked out loud.

Carli did not want to call Buck again, especially after the electricity issue, and she durn sure wasn't going to call the sheriff or talk to Thelma at Dispatch. Nathan had already helped her out of a jam once this week. And the thought of calling Lank made her heart pound. She was on her own.

Bouncing across the pasture, steering around

clumps of yucca and bunches of dried tumbleweeds, the truck followed the winding creek bed. Snow covered hills rose gently on either side, blocking her view of the pasture.

A lone cow watched as she approached. Nosing a clump of snow piled in front of a mass of yucca, it was strange the animal was so intent on that one spot and refused to leave. Carli noticed the color of the snow was more dirty than white. That's when something twitched causing bits of snow to flutter in the air. It looked like an ear had popped up. Carli stopped the truck and walked closer.

"You had a baby." The new momma cow looked at her with dark, soft eyes, then leaned her head down and nudged the lump again but it didn't move.

Carli stopped. Was it alive? She was certain she had seen that ear move. And why was there a new calf already? Buck said they were months away from birthing time. She took off her gloves, knelt down beside it, and stuck her fingers in his mouth. The newborn calf's tongue felt scratchy and cold. She felt a slight wiggle, or did she imagine it? He was alive, but near frozen.

Remembering that this baby had a protective and nervous mother nearby, Carli glanced over her shoulder. The big black Angus cow watched patiently. Carli needed to warm up the baby. If she drove all the way back to headquarters, hitched the trailer up to haul both mother and calf, she wondered how much longer the calf would be alive. She noted the cow's ear tag number. "I'll be right back with your baby."

She ran to the truck, dumped a pile of cake to keep the mother occupied, and opened the passenger side door. Kneeling down next to the little newborn, she scooped him up in both arms. Heavier than she thought, he was solid but not many hours old. A bull calf, the cord still hung from his belly. She hoisted him up into the seat and closed the door.

The newest citizen of the Wild Cow Ranch was motionless on the leather seat. Carli turned the heat on high. Her fingers tingled from the cold and her arms ached from carrying the calf; he was heavier than he looked, maybe sixty pounds. She pulled into her driveway and hurried to open the front door, leaving it ajar.

She gently lifted the calf from the vehicle and then realized she needed something on the floor for the baby to lie on. Carrying him inside and placing him in the entry hall, she hurried through the kitchen to the hall cabinet to find material to make a pallet. She chose a faded blanket, and soon had him moved to his new bed, although it was only temporary.

Peeling off layers of clothing, the warmth of the house felt good on her skin.

Quietly on his side, the calf was not moving. His eyes closed and his muzzle felt cold. She pulled his pallet closer to the wall heater. What did she have that could warm him up fast? She wandered through the house looking for a small heater. Maybe another blanket? Her blow dryer. Why not? She needed an extension cord too.

With the heat on low, she massaged and blew the calf's wet hair. He was sopping wet from the snow blanket that had covered him and thawed out in the feed truck.

In the back of her mind, she remembered a dinner conversation between Buck and Lank about a concoction used to feed calves that might be born early. Sometimes snowstorms brought pregnancies on sooner, and it was hard on the babies born during a cold front. "Papa's Firewater," Buck had called it. Carli had no idea why that stuck in her mind, she had barely paid attention, but the ingredients soon came to her.

In a large mixing bowl, she stirred a little milk, two eggs, and one cup of coffee, leftover from breakfast. She crunched up six aspirins in a small bowl and stirred that into the mixture. Since he was cold, she heated this on the stove for just a few minutes. Now she needed something to get the stuff into the calf's throat. "Thank you, Grandma," Carli said out loud after digging through a kitchen drawer and finding a syringe. Of course. Every cattle ranch probably kept one of these on hand.

Holding the calf's head, she squirted the mixture into his mouth holding his tongue out of the way. As the warm liquid reached the back of his throat, he swallowed. Carli hoped that was a good sign. The baby coughed but his eyes were still closed.

She picked up the blow dryer and kept running it over his hair, combing it with her fingers as the device blew the warm air around him. Suddenly big, brown eyes fluttered open, and he strained to raise his head. Carli's heart jumped with joy. He was going to live. She scratched the black curls in the middle of his forehead.

"Let's get you back to your momma because I'll

bet, you're hungry." He actually made a little grunt.

She carried him out to the truck and headed towards the pasture to look for cow number 336. As she approached the cattle guard, a lone cow bawled at the sight of the feed truck. Sure enough. It was his momma. She must have followed the feed truck for as far as she could. Carli stopped right next to her, picked up the calf one more time and set him down by her nose. The cow sniffed and began licking her baby who raised his wobbly head and let out a weak bawl. Momma nudged his backside, urging him to stand. He finally managed to balance on all four wobbly feet. His appetite got the best of him as he searched under the Angus cow for the end that would give him his dinner. And then he latched on.

"Yay!" Carli jumped with excitement. She had handled the situation all by herself and successfully reunited momma and baby.

Carli was exhausted and starved, and the day was almost over. But she was grateful to have witnessed life triumphing over death and to know she had a hand in the outcome.

Chapter Twenty-Five

Friday Morning, Day 5 Alone

The morning dawned clear and chilly. Carli stood on her front porch inhaling the crisp air deeply until her lungs stung and her nose tingled. She exhaled and watched her breath swirl in gray puffs around her face, and pulled her woolen cap down over her ears. The quiet of the Texas Panhandle always surprised her. Despite the peaceful promise of a new day, she was more than ready to be relieved of her obligations. It had been a ridiculous week.

When her ranch help returned, Carli would do what she always did on Christmas Eve and Christmas Day. Nothing. Just another day. In Georgia she would have thrown simple ingredients together into the slow cooker for Chicken Alfredo, her favorite comfort food next to mac 'n' cheese, and then she'd have ridden and worked with Beau and her clients' horses. Nothing spectacular ever happened for the holiday. But this was her first Christmas in

Texas, not that she expected any great hoopla, or spiritual revelation for that matter.

Lola and Buck had invited her to their church for Christmas Eve services. He said they would hear about the birth of baby Jesus and have a potluck supper. She was still so new to the concept of having a Lord and Savior that she wasn't too sure she wanted to be around a huge room full of strangers.

Since her guardians, the Fitzgeralds, had died, she never thought much of Christmas as being different from any other day of the year. They were an older couple when she went to live with them as a baby, so the holidays were never a huge deal that brought back lots of memories. Usually, a small tabletop tree and a new toy for her. She remembered the aroma of baked ham and sweet potatoes, but certainly nothing related to religion or Jesus. There hadn't been much celebration any time of the year growing up. The Fitzgeralds were low key. Carli had lived a quiet existence, and the curiosity about her birth family eventually faded like a misty dream. Although the sting of her mother abandoning her had eventually eased, the unanswered questions about her heritage were never far from her thoughts.

Her grandparents, Jean and Ward, had no information about Carli's whereabouts, and her mother Michelle did not seek her out to visit for any holidays. Why had she never asked the Fitzgeralds about her mother? And now Carli lived in her grandparents' house where her mother grew up. She felt Michelle's presence even stronger. She couldn't help but wonder what made the pregnant teen run away and give up her baby to strangers.

Carli sighed. Christmas would be just another day of chores for her, but today she was going on a ride. Another day spent alone was nothing new over the course of her life, but she had to admit she was beginning to get used to having her ranch foreman and his wife around. They seemed to genuinely care about her and about the Wild Cow Ranch.

Beau stretched his neck over the pipe rail and gave her a nicker of greeting, his breath fogging white from his nose. She smiled. He followed her along the fence line to the gate like an oversized, lumbering puppy dog. She loved how his coat shined.

"How about a ride today?" she murmured. She had waited until midmorning, after the sun burned off some of the chill from the night before. Ride several hours, finish up with the chores, and then her ranch supervisory duties would be done. That was her plan for the day anyway. Everybody would be back safe and sound at headquarters by tomorrow evening. She wondered about Lank. They hadn't spoken for almost a week, since lunch last Saturday when she had rudely brought up how much she hated this time of year, not realizing it was Lank's first Christmas without his mother. It was really insensitive of her. Instead of wallowing in her own pity and regrets, she made a vow to be more aware of her employees and their needs. He had left before she could apologize.

Finding the axe in the saddle house, she busted the ice in all the pens and then whistled. The horses were gathered around a hay bale down the hill from where she stood in the corral. Ears perked, heads lifted, they ambled towards her.

She filled one feed trough with oats and let Beau munch on the treat while she gathered her riding gear. He swung his head around to glance as she brushed his back and then again when she walked in his direction with the saddle pad but ignored her as she placed it on him. Before she went back for the saddle and bridle, Carli took a few minutes to rub Lank's new horse Phoenix who watched intently, almost as if he was wondering if he was going to work today or not.

"Okay, I'll give you some too." Returning with a coffee can full of oats for Phoenix, Carli watched as he greedily buried his nose in the feed and blew, scattering chafe on the ground. Several other ranch horses gathered at the fence to watch from a pen away. "I'll take care of you guys when I get back."

After Lank's horse died in the hay barn fire, he bought Phoenix, a bay gelding, from the Rafter O Ranch. The night of the fire was so awful, one of the most terrifying for Carli. Goosebumps rose on her arms when she thought about it. She could've lost Beau and Lank. Buck, too. Such destruction and so much fear. But it also turned out to be a night of restoration that changed her life. Maybe there really was a God after all.

The registered quarter horse Phoenix came from one of the Olsen's award-winning cutting horses, and looked different from Lank's other horse, Blackie. It was better he didn't have the constant reminder of the horse that he had raised from a colt. A lump formed in Carli's throat when she thought about poor Blackie and how he must've suffered. Carli prayed nothing like that would ever happen again. Phoenix was cute, and smart too. Lank had worked with him a good bit and was happy with the horse's progress. He'd make a good addition to the Wild Cow's remuda.

With Beau saddled, Carli led him through the gate, latching it behind her. Then swung her legs over the saddle and clicked her tongue, asking him to trot. She smiled at the thought of her life changes on this Texas ranch. Although she had ridden Western as well as English at Georgia horse shows, this was different. This was real, not for show competition. Here, she felt like a true cowgirl.

They were going to take a ride through the little heifers. None of them were due to give birth yet, it would be another few months, but she wanted to check for runny noses and wheezy coughs. Trotting up the small hill to the trap, she nudged Beau closer to the next gate.

Chapter Twenty-Six

Friday Morning, Heifer Pasture

Carli steered Beau closer to the gate so she could latch it, and then they stopped at the top of a hill. The Wild Cow Ranch extended out into a scrubby beige world mile after mile for as far as she could see. In another direction, gently sloping hills rose to meet the sky, covered in more sand-colored dry grass and clumps of brown yucca leaves. Thoughts of her old place and Georgia came into mind. Trees. That's what she missed the most. Trees and dense bushes, mossy rocks and a living landscape, gently trickling water, and the clean smell of a breathing forest.

The part of Texas she had inherited was dry and bland, treeless and stark, yet it had its own beauty. You couldn't walk in a day for as far as your eyes could see. While the landscape held no color this time of year, the Texas sky made up for it. The clouds were ever-changing in a canopy that extended forever, with sunrises and sunsets displaying a myriad of color combinations. Every day was new living under a different sky. And there was no better country to raise cattle. This is where her roots were. She had to admit she was looking forward to her first spring and summer in this place.

Carli looked over the heifers, most of which were gathered around the water tank and the hay bale feeders. She got a good count. Everybody was there so she decided to ride on into the next pasture.

The sun beat down on her back and it felt good. It was an unbelievably beautiful day for December, especially since last night was below freezing. Meadowlarks called out to each other on both sides of her as she rode through their surround-sound of melody. She focused on their tune and the view. Topping the next small rise, a shallow, treeless valley stretched for miles until the end faded into a blur on the horizon under a sky of cerulean blue. A peacefulness settled over her heart. She sincerely believed now in a Creator for no human could have made all of this beautiful nature.

A windmill stood in the middle of a low valley perfectly frozen in motion like a giant stick figure. Not a breeze was stirring, which was strange for Texas. Red Angus cattle turned their faces to watch her ride by and then continued their drinking. Before long, her head got too hot. She crammed her woolen cap into a pocket of her goose down coat. If this continued, she'd have to peel off one of her many layers.

Wondering what the high would be for today, she reached around and realized her phone was missing from her hip pocket. For just a second panic hit and she stopped Beau to search other pockets, thinking it must've fallen out. Instead of her cell, she pulled out a half-eaten power bar. And then she remembered that she had needed to plug the phone in last night. Her cell still lay on the kitchen counter, recharging. She didn't want to stop riding though to head back.

The day was too perfect. She nudged Beau onward as he picked his way around the clumps of yucca. Clearing her head, she just focused on Beau's plodding hooves. Sun and a big Texas sky made her troubles seem miles away. Her previous life in Georgia, so different than now, seemed like a far away dream.

At the next windmill she dismounted and let her horse get a good drink. She took off her glove and reached for the thermos clipped to a ring on the saddle. Cool water trickled down the back of her throat. She drank deeply and tightened the lid. At least she remembered water. She couldn't refill the thermos though because there was no wind. The pipe spout that usually trickled water from deep below into the stock tank was dry.

As they emerged from the bottom of the valley, Carli noticed a bank of clouds on the horizon. Dark gray and deep purple, they looked ominous but were miles away. She had learned that things seemed closer here in the Texas Panhandle. What might be a notable landmark on the horizon could actually take a half day's ride on horseback to reach. The clouds didn't worry her. The sun was still shining hot and bright. When they got to the next windmill, she might have to take off her coat and tie it around her waist.

They continued on and, since she didn't have

her phone, time wasn't a concern. The pasture they rode in comprised several sections. She focused on the rhythm of Beau's power under the saddle as she nudged him into a lope across the grasslands. Her mind cleared. She calmly breathed in and out, time standing still. How many minutes, or hours, went by? She didn't know and she didn't care. Without her phone, she couldn't check the time.

Carli never got a chance to take off her coat because the building storm bank kicked up a sudden breeze straight from the north. Her cheeks felt the warmth of the sun but the icy gust from behind chilled her ears. Reaching back for her woolen cap, she discovered it had fallen out of her coat pocket. That's when she decided to turn Beau around and head back in the direction of headquarters.

A windmill on her far left, she steered him towards it. Dismounting, she checked her pockets again for something that was obviously not there. The wind had kicked up, the blades turned and squeaked in the northern breeze. She filled the water bottle from the spout as the mill pumped up fresh water from below. Beau stood next to the water trough but didn't drink. He had enough at the one before. Carli watched his raised head, eyes staring, ears moving forward and back, listening, maybe for the impending storm.

By the time she mounted again, the wind had completely erased any of the warmth from just moments before. Her nose and ears tingled as she turned up the collar of her goose down. She didn't have to encourage Beau to move. He felt a little skittish to her as though he was anxious to get back to his barn and away from the threatening weather.

Not sure when it started, but she suddenly noticed small, white specks of snow circling her head. She squeezed her legs, made the smooching sound, and urged Beau into a lope. They rode north and she pressed her eyes shut against the cold. Icy sleet stung her face as she encouraged Beau into the wind. She had to pull on the reins and stop long enough to swipe the moisture from her face, then turn her head out of the gale so she could take a breath.

Carli hadn't lived on the Wild Cow Ranch that long and she wasn't really sure of the lay of the land. She thought she might be in what they called the Middle Pasture, but how far from headquarters she wasn't sure; she hadn't paid attention to that on her ride. How many gates had she opened and gone through? People claim that animals can always find their way home, but Beau wasn't familiar with this sprawling place either. Plus, the wind and snow made visibility impossible and could confuse his sense of direction.

Suddenly, the small ice turned into fat flakes that stuck to her hair and covered Beau's mane. Her chest tightened and her breath came short as she tried to inhale. The frigid wind hurt her throat. She stopped. Turning Beau to face south and with their backs against the cold blast she tried to think. She caught her breath. Why would she ride away from headquarters?

She turned him back towards north and home. The snow was coming in sideways, fat and wet. It was almost impossible to ride into the icy bluster.

The storm howled and changed before she felt it. It whipped the tops of the cottonwoods that clumped in the low washout around a spring. Suddenly the force hit her face with a startling, cold blast. The gusts kicked up another notch as the snow kept coming in sideways.

"Whoa, boy." She pulled gently on Beau's reins and stopped to settle her mind and think. How far had they gone? She had no idea. The quickest way is a straight line, but they were losing daylight fast. Soon they'd have no sun or horizon to guide them. She focused on stilling her heart. Think, Carli.

Then she remembered a barn across the fence line next to the windmill they had just passed. They could seek shelter there for a few hours until this blew over, give Beau and her some rest, and then hoof it back home as soon as there was a break in the wind. She turned him around and loped back to the windmill which blurred like a mirage until they got closer. With the wind at her back, her face still tingled but at least she could open her eyes. She hesitated. Why in the world would she ride away from headquarters in the middle of a snowstorm? But she could barely see her hand in front of her face and the wind was relentless.

Stopping at the wire gate, she wondered if this was a gate into her pasture or a neighbor's place. Carli dismounted to open it and then led her horse through. She turned to remount and noticed icicles hanging from Beau's nose. The sight strengthened her resolve to get them both to shelter fast. The dilapidated barn stood in a haze of white. She sure wished she had her cap.

Chapter Twenty-Seven

Friday Afternoon, Wild Cow Ranch Pasture

Carli steered her horse Beau towards the gray image of a structure barely visible through the blinding snow. Before she reached shelter, the snow turned to sleet, bits of ice that pelted her jacket and stung her face. The storm had officially turned into a norther. She'd read about those. Blinding sheets of ice blowing in sideways and blocking her view, making her squint. From the gate, she led her horse, but she could barely make out the barn just ahead. Without her cap, her ears were frozen and probably about to drop off any second. They ached. With a best guess as to the structure's opening, they moved forward.

Beau plodded along, seemingly in no hurry. Always calm in whatever situation they found themselves and always willing to do whatever Carli asked. Her heart tightened at the thought he might be suffering.

She guessed right. The entrance emerged like a black hole. Beau picked up the pace next to her, as if he finally caught on to her plan. Too weary to find the next gate, she led him through a break in the rail fence stepping over a broken wooden slat.

As they entered, the sting of sleet on her face ended, thank God. She stomped her boots to shake the snow loose. The wall facing north was windowless and solid. She and Beau would at least have three sides of shelter. And more importantly, against that north wall stood a pile of natural insulation. Stacks of square bales went from floor to ceiling.

The open side of the structure offered a view of total whiteness, as if she were trapped inside a cloud. Despite the storm, afternoon light somehow filtered through and turned the slashing ice a dull gray. A roaring cloud hovered, as the wind whistled and rattled what was left of the old barn. It had stood for many years and survived countless windstorms. "Please hold it together for one more night, Lord," Carli whispered into the gloom. As soon as the storm eased, she and Beau would hightail it home.

Tugging the saddle and blanket off her horse, she rubbed him down with handfuls of dry straw that littered the ground. At first, she thought the haystack might be too old and moldy, but on closer inspection it seemed good. She broke off a half-flake for Beau, placing it right in front of the larger stack and pulled him closer. She'd have to make sure he didn't overeat. Eating strange hay from what he was used to could make him sick, but she thought it looked okay. She wouldn't give him much at first. Better to go slow.

Right behind him, Carli sat cross-legged on the lower edge of the higher stack that reached to the ceiling and covered her lap with the scratchy side of the horse's saddle blanket. She took a sip of water from what was left in her bottle and munched on the last half of the protein bar she had discovered earlier. Finally, she pulled her goose down jacket over her head and closed the front around her face. Warmth washed over her stinging, raw nose and cheeks. She sighed. Her arms were at a strained angle, but she decided she could survive that until her head warmed up.

And then Nature called.

"You have got to be kidding me." Beau's ears moved at the sound of her voice, but otherwise he ignored her as he ate. She sat there as long as she could, her face cocooned in the warmth of her coat, until she couldn't stay still one more second. Hurrying over to the far corner, the cold reached right through Carli's core when she squatted as if she had no coat at all.

In a flash she was back on the hay bale, just as frozen as she'd been before. Back to square one but this time no snack and she dare not take even one more sip of water.

She had never felt teeth-chattering cold like this before. How long can a human body withstand a snowstorm? Would they find her Christmas Eve frozen solid, her faithful horse munching hay at the side of her rigid body? Would her precious Beau be frozen stiff like a stuffed Trigger? As usual, her imagination created more drama than she could ever deal with.

The reality was that she'd spend another holiday

alone. Nothing new there but holed up in this barn while a snowstorm blew recklessly around her made her wonder if this would be the last Christmas she'd ever have to face.

Is this your plan, God? Is this what you had in mind for me? Inherit a ranch, move to Texas, and then freeze to death? Great.

This would keep the folks in Dixon talking for another generation or two. Ward and Jean's granddaughter didn't know a thing about cows, and it was just as well because a High Plains norther is what did her in.

An ache settled in the back of her throat and moisture bubbled in her eyes. Crying? Sure, that always solves the problem.

She'd been on her own in this world since her guardians had died, alone to figure things out. Nothing to cry over, that was her life. She'd accepted it. But now she had so much she wanted to learn and do. This ranch, Jean and Ward's legacy, had given her a new life. A place where she belonged. After all the hardships she had faced, the thing that was going to end it all was some stupid ice and snowstorm. Unbelievable.

Her mind churned with turmoil and confusion as shivers ran through her body. She stood to stomp her feet and get the feeling back into her legs. Every joint hurt. Her toes stung with every step. She swung her arms managing a few jumping jacks to get her blood pumping, and was reminded again how much she missed her woolen cap.

The wind blew furiously. Relentlessly. The sleet kept coming sideways driven by the wind. Hard and fast and angry. She refused to believe this was the end. The aggravation of the week and the pent-up frustration at herself for getting caught in a storm would surely make her head explode at any second. But she refused to cry.

"Why am I here? What do You want of me?" She screamed into the wall of gray. Her horse turned soft eyes in her direction, obviously unfazed by the emotional outburst. Carli turned and plopped back down on hay bales, pulled her knees to her chest, and balanced the horse blanket against her. Pulling her goose down coat over her head again, she held the front together with gloved hands. Resting her head on her knees, she focused on breathing the warm air generated by her mini jacket-tent, willing herself not to cry.

Ranch owners don't cry. Nathan had just talked about that.

Why do women cry more than men? Or so it seemed.

What was she doing here? "If I'm where You want me, then guide me onward. Don't let this be the end." Her throat ached from unshed tears. "Do you hear me, God?" she sputtered, her whispers lost in the moaning wind. A strong gust rattled the old wood. She just knew the entire wall would come down on top of her at any minute.

She was losing it. Christmas. Trapped in a norther. She was having a nervous breakdown in the middle of nowhere. Definitely not carrying on the family's ranching tradition and making the Jameson name proud. What was wrong with her?

Why did she hate this time of year most of all? Maybe it was easier to ignore it. She didn't have to think about how truly alone she felt, particularly after her guardians, the Fitzgeralds, had both passed away. She'd always been the responsible one, acting like an adult way before her years. Forced to take care of herself in so many ways. Her life had been filled with work and horses, the one thing she was passionate about. No trips. No real friends. A dull existence. Predictable.

At least this was a new adventure. Nothing boring about freezing to death. Carli squeezed her eyes shut. Too cold to sleep, the noise of the wind rattled the tin sides. Somewhere wood thumped and squeaked, maybe a fence. Nothing to do but endure the inner thoughts swirling in her head just like the norther outside.

Suddenly she realized it was the celebrations she was never a part of that had bugged her. No memories of Christmases. No mother. No grandparents. That's what made her sad the most. Her mother abandoning her and robbing her of a real family. The Fitzgeralds did the best they could. She couldn't really complain about them. They weren't cruel by any means, but they were elderly, reclusive, and most of their family was dead. Plus, that wasn't her family.

That was the problem. The scenes of everybody else's Christmas overwhelmed her. All the presents, feelings of warm fuzzies, family dinners, and people who really want you around. She had none of that. And she hated her mother Michelle for it. But then she thought about how Buck told her to consider looking at Christmas in a different way. It was the season of renewed hope, thinking about the blessings from the previous year, and considering a

God that was bigger than anything we controlled. A God who blessed us and guided us, if we let Him.

Definitely her life had changed over the past few months. And she sensed something different inside. She was tired of feeling like a victim and didn't want to feel sorry for herself anymore. And, if she was being honest, that's exactly what she was doing. Sure, she'd had kind of a tough life. Left to fend for herself. No fairy tale family. No magazine-perfect Christmas celebrations. But everyone in this life has a story. Some easy, some hard, happy or sad. Some people have endured terrible tragedies. Some had debilitating diseases or disabilities.

I'm young, healthy, and I own a ranch, for gosh sakes. Who am I to be sad about my life? Maybe it's time to start new and change my attitude.

Bundled under the horse blanket and her jacket, she was suddenly so tired, so sleepy. She thought of her Grandma Jean. She had been one tough lady. A champion rodeo rider. Yet, as far as what Carli heard from some townspeople, Jean also had a kind heart. And she loved Christmas. She baked tons of cookies and invited neighbors to witness the ranch's Christmas lights. She brought happiness to them, blessed them, shared a special holiday with them.

As Carli drifted into dreamland, she thought, I've got her genes, her DNA. I could be like her, open up the ranch, decorate for Christmas. I could enjoy Christmas. Start new memories.

Suddenly a peace came over her troubled mind. Storms don't last forever. This is where I want you. You're home.

What was that? Her own thoughts? A voice? A

calm warmth enveloped her even though outside it was below freezing. Her eyes snapped open. This storm will be over soon.

Wiping moisture from her cheek, somehow, she knew in her heart that she and Beau would be all right. God wouldn't let life defeat her. He was with her. The tears that suddenly leaked from her eyes were not of fear, but of joy and hope. As soon as this storm passes and the sun breaks through the clouds, like she knew it would, she'd ride back to ranch headquarters. And she'd finally be home. Ready to make new memories. To start over.

Chapter Twenty-Eight

Lank watched his nephews act out what had become known as the "bear tackle" for the one hundredth time. They each took turns being the bear, and then the other one would tackle him down resulting in snarls and a tangle of arms and legs. His sister had finally said enough on Thursday evening and put them to bed but not before Lank had to recount the story one more time. The minute they woke this morning the boys were at it again. Lank watched and laughed.

"Coffee's ready," said Kelly. "And I give up. This is going to be a topic of conversation at our house for many months to come." She placed two coffee mugs on the table and collapsed in a chair.

"Surely they'll wind down after a day or two, won't they?" Lank sipped the hot coffee and made a face.

"You don't like coffee, do you? I forgot. How about some iced tea?"

"That would be better." He never had acquired a taste for coffee, but the smell reminded him of his childhood home. That along with roasting chilis and the doughy smell of fresh tortillas. His parents drank coffee every morning and afternoon.

Kelly piled his plate with scrambled eggs and sausage.

"Come on boys. Eat some breakfast," she said.

Just as he dug in, Carli's face flashed before him. She hadn't called him all week and he couldn't help but wonder how things were going.

"I should get back to the Wild Cow today," he said.

Kelly sat down next to him. "Is there any way you can go with us to see Santa? The SPCA is having their annual fundraiser. We're taking our dogs and getting our pictures made."

"Please, Uncle Lank."

"Go with us."

"I want you in the picture," said Kelly.

Lank knew he'd lost the argument before it began. Of course, he couldn't miss the chance to have his picture made with his nephews, sister and husband, their dogs, and Santa. For a brief second, he thought of Carli which brought a stab to his heart. He wanted her at his side with his family.

The rest of the morning was a whirl of Kelly getting everybody ready. Coordinating sweaters and bandana scarfs for their two dogs, a beagle and a German Shepherd. Zane wanted to take his stuffed bear. Lank had one clean shirt left, a bright blue but his sister nixed that. She dug through Matt's closet and found a green sweater. Lank put it on reluctantly, but he was going to leave his cowboy hat on for the picture. That was a fact.

During all the frenzy Carli's face kept sifting

in and out of his thoughts. He picked up his phone to dial her number half a dozen times, but never completed the call. His mother would have said that's God talking. When a thought keeps bugging you, it's probably the Holy Spirit guiding us to our purpose. Lank had never put much thought into what his purpose might be and why God would even care. He loved being on horseback and he loved working cows. As far as doing anything else in life, he wasn't interested. But he'd never thought about God guiding him with relationships to people. Why was Carli on his mind all day?

Lank stepped outside onto the front porch. With a heavy sigh, he finally dialed Carli's number while his sister tried to load their dogs into the car. No answer. That was strange. She never got far from her phone; even when she went riding, she always had it in her back pocket.

"Load up, guys. Matt's meeting us there," Kelly said. They all piled into the car.

The city park overflowed with people and pets dressed up in their holiday best. It was fortunate that the weather was mild and there wasn't an icy wind blowing. In fact, the air felt more like a spring day than December. Under the gazebo, the Santa Claus sat in an oversized throne chair surrounded by flocked Christmas trees and helpers in green tights with red jumpsuits. While they waited in line, Lank kept dialing Carli.

He paused to consider calling Buck too but hated to cause any worry. He felt sure Buck had enough on his hands in Dallas. The big city was not his favorite place, and he felt sure Lola had them going everywhere.

Lank smiled for the camera, refusing to take off his hat even when Kelly shot him an icy glare. But she had enough on her hands with dogs and kids, and Matt arriving just in time. That done, they had a lengthy discussion about burgers or pizza. Pizza won. Lank was without his own wheels, so he settled into the car. They'd have to drop the dogs off first, and then go to dinner. He dialed Carli at least ten more times.

By the time they pulled into the driveway, snow flurries were swirling overhead, and the streets were dusted with a layer of white. Lank could not shake Carli from his head, the urgency to call her number again burned like a hot poker.

"I've got to get back to the ranch," he said as they walked in the front door.

Kelly turned to him with a gasp. "You're not leaving in this storm. It's supposed to snow all night."

"All the more reason I should be there in the morning. Thanks for everything. It's been fun." He leaned in to give her a peck on the cheek.

"Call me the minute you get home," she said. "Promise."

"I will." Lank hurried to the spare bedroom and crammed everything into his bag. "If I forgot anything, just let me know."

Before stepping outside, he turned to his sister. "Love you, Sis." His voice broke. "I know you miss her and I'm sorry to be leaving."

Tears shimmered in Kelly's eyes. "I love you too, little brother. Thanks for being here this week. It meant more to me than you'll ever know."

"Y'all are coming out for Christmas Eve dinner, right? Lola is cooking and you know there'll be plenty."

"If this storm doesn't close the roads, we'll be there," Kelly said.

Even the nephews begging him to watch a movie with them didn't faze his purpose. He had a strong urge to be at the ranch now, and he wasn't going to ignore it. Matt walked him out to his pickup truck.

"If you get in a bind, call me. Drive safe, man." Matt patted Lank's shoulder.

"I think I'm leaving early enough to beat the worst of it." Lank backed out of the drive, his hands gripping the steering wheel.

The houses shielded most of the blowing snow from the city streets. It wasn't bad until he got out on the interstate where semi-trucks had pulled over to wait out the worst of it. The wind gusts rocked his pickup truck, and he had to lower his speed, but he kept moving. The road was snow packed, but not a solid ice sheet. Yet.

As he turned off the interstate to the rural road, the traffic diminished but the wind and accumulation of snow never let up. By the time he got to the caliche dirt road that led to the ranch, he doubted he could make it up the hill from the draw. He tried and failed. The hill was too steep, his tires unable to grip the snow-packed road. At least a foot of snow had fallen, with drifts over three feet in some places. He'd have to go back around and through Dixon, which added at least another forty-five minutes and, in this storm, maybe even longer.

His stomach was tied in knots with worry over why he hadn't been able to reach Carli all day. He couldn't even begin to imagine what might have happened. Well, he could think of a list of a million things that could go wrong on a ranch, but he refused to think in specifics.

He had to get home.

Chapter Twenty-Nine

Warm and snug in the hay. Or was that Carli's imagination? Maybe she was just numb, frozen. Still sounded like the norther was blowing out there fast and furiously. "I must've dozed a little." Beau turned his head towards the sound of her voice. "Hey, boy, you doing okay?"

She had to stretch out of her frozen, pretzel-like position. And now that she had, she realized it was all in her mind about being warm. Dang, she was freezing. She stood, went to Beau and hugged his furry body which wasn't exactly warm either. He was cold but didn't seem to be suffering. Please, God, we've got to get out of here. Send us help.

The tin roof shimmied and swayed. With one wall open to the elements, how long could this old structure stand? How long could she and Beau hang on?

Carli got back into her cocoon, bringing the saddle blanket over her chest and tucking the hay all around her. A shiver ran through her from head to toe and her breathing became slow and shallow.

She had never been this cold before. Her nose and cheeks burned, and her fingers ached. Her eyes stung and she felt so sleepy. Maybe that ranch hand will find them. Where was he anyway? His name escaped her. She tried to remember, but her eyes grew so heavy she had to close them. She wouldn't be able to stay awake much longer.

The wood slats creaked. Her eyes snapped open. She worried that the whipping wind would tear the whole structure down, with her and Beau inside. Tornados wreaked havoc all over the country. Certainly, northers destroyed property. Probably people too.

Suddenly, a figure flashed across the open side of the haybarn. Was that a person running? Who in the world would be out in this storm? Maybe they had finally come for her.

"Lank? Is that you? We're in here." That was his name. She surprised herself that his was the name she'd called out. Why did I think of him? Why not Nathan?

That probably wasn't a person, just snow flying sideways, more howling wind that sounded like screaming. She realized she had watched too many scary movies over the years, Abominable Snowman and all that. Was she getting hypothermia? Was it affecting her brain?

No sooner had she almost let her mind go down a dark path of thinking the worst, her ranch foreman, Buck, came to mind. She must be delirious again because it was like he was in that old barn with her, giving her a Bible lesson. His words swarmed in her mind.

"God doesn't want us to be afraid. He doesn't

want us to think about the evil things of this world. In fact, in Second Timothy it says, 'For God hath not given us the spirit of fear; but of power, and of love, and of a sound mind.' You can choose love and good things rather than being afraid and sad."

How can he remember all those verses? She wondered if she would ever learn how to do that.

And no, she didn't want to be sad anymore. She didn't want to be afraid to get close to people. What kind of life would that be? She could almost imagine herself older, living alone, keeping her distance from everyone. God, please help me to be more open and trusting of people. I don't want to be alone.

She felt herself slipping in and out of consciousness. Not really dreams. More like rambling thoughts as she struggled to make sense of her life. Some moments were so real, like when it seemed Buck was right there beside her.

As she shivered from her makeshift mini-cave in the hay, she languidly watched the opening and spaced out on the furious zig zags of the sleet and snowflakes. There went another figure running by. Or was it really? She wasn't afraid this time. In fact, the form took on the shape of someone she had seen in a photo in her house—her Grandma Jean in her rodeo outfit, turquoise boots, red scarf. The shape stopped and looked right at Carli and spoke tenderly.

"Oh, Carli, we love you. So glad you're at the Wild Cow taking care of it for us. You'll do a great job. We know you can do it. When you get home there's so much you can do. Let the past go. Don't let it burden you. Choose happiness. And when Christmas comes, invite the community. Bake cookies. String up a million lights. Blind the darkness, the evil. Let His light shine!"

Then, like a movie reel, Carli saw in her mind's eye what the ranch at Christmas time would look like—all decorated. She imagined Belinda, Lola, and her baking cookies, laughing, tasting, flinging a little flour at each other.

Outside, Buck and Lank strung lights along the fences, around bushes, and up and down every nook and cranny of the barns and houses. The whole place was illuminated like a theme park. Trucks and cars were parked all over and crowds of people strolled to take it all in. Kids laughed and ran to watch a mechanical Santa with reindeer that flew across a rooftop.

Grandma Jean spoke again. "Help others, Carli. So many are less fortunate. It's easy to share happiness with them. Just choose to do so. Don't keep it all to yourself. Watch them smile as they enjoy the lights or taste your cookies."

Carli rolled over in the scratchy hay and extended her arm towards her grandmother. She wanted to touch her, to be held by her. Was she real?

But the image faded like smoke.

"Grandma...I'm not such a good cook."

Why did she have to think about cookies? Gosh, she was hungry. Sugar cookies with red and green sprinkles. Star shapes. Christmas tree shapes. Heart shapes. Maybe she could find old cookie cutters in the kitchen that had belonged to her grandmother.

Perhaps hunger, and of course the cold, were both playing tricks on her mind. She just needed to get home, to feel warmth. She worried about Beau and constantly looked to him. He seemed okay. But he'd be better off in his warm barn.

"Lord, help us please." Her whispered prayer was muted by the howling wind.

The sleet was swirling outside the barn. Carli stared, mesmerized by its patterns. Another shape. She knew it couldn't be a person. That's what her head told her. But as a tear slid down her face her heart prompted her to think of her mother, Michelle. Blonde hair flying in the wind. Familiar eyes staring at Carli. The same hazel eyes that Carli saw in the mirror every morning. But no words. Not one word from the woman who had given her life.

Why had Michelle not wanted to know her daughter? And how could Carli ever forgive her? She knew Buck, God, everyone would tell her to forgive so she could set the burden down that she was carrying. Set it down so she could be free and get on with her life. Without forgiveness she was in a prison of her own making.

She couldn't do it. Not yet. Maybe someday. But not this day.

Why didn't her mother say anything to her? The woman remained motionless, staring, and then disappeared into the fog of swirling white.

"Please come back," Carli mumbled as she yielded to the sobs that shook her.

Chapter Thirty

Lank Torres pulled into ranch headquarters and parked in front of his double-wide trailer. "Shoot, forgot to leave a light on." He fumbled for the key ring in his pocket, suddenly realizing how dark it had become.

His house sat on the backside of the compound under a clump of old elm trees. He liked it here. Out of sight from the main road and it was an easy walk to the saddle house.

He tucked his chin into the collar of his jacket and stumbled against the blowing snow. Apparently, Lola and Buck weren't back as the second floor of the cookhouse where their apartment was located was dark. The glow of their television usually flickered through the window every evening.

The corral light hadn't been turned on either. Fingers struggling to find the right key, he finally stepped inside, stomping the snow off his boots.

He looked through the small window over his bed. Carli's house was dark too. Some nights he lay in bed staring at the light shining from the guest room that she now occupied in Jean and Ward's house. He always knew when she called it a night. Then he could rest easy too.

With a deep sigh, he realized how weary he felt but knew he wouldn't sleep. This holiday had done him in. Those nephews were nonstop energy. And Lank never imagined last Christmas would be the final one with his mother. If he had known, he would've stayed at the hospital more, even if it meant the end of his job at the Wild Cow. But he and his sis had tag-teamed, taking turns watching their mother get better and then worse, then much better, and then gone.

He braced himself for the cold again to unload his stuff from the truck, which wasn't much since he had left in a whirl of emotion. He stumbled on the flat rocks that formed a sidewalk to his front door. Not sure why, but it had been urgent for him to be any place but here and he needed to see his sister. Watching Nathan convince Carli to spend Christmas Day at the Rafter O with the Olsens hadn't helped his mood any.

It was dark. Too dark. Something kept niggling at his mind. Grabbing his heavy canvas coat, which hung on the hook in the narrow hall, Lank wandered out to the corral to turn on the light. The saddle house door was unlocked. Carli missed it, which meant it had probably been unlocked all week. He knew Buck and Lola went to visit their niece, but he put it out of his mind, only to be reminded this afternoon when Buck called asking if he was back at the ranch and if he'd heard anything from Carli. She had called Buck about the power being off. Lank didn't mention it, but he doubted Carli would ever call him again after the way she and Nathan had been eyeing each other on shipping day.

He squinted his eyes in the sudden brightness of the tack room. The wind rattled the tin sides. Tree branches scratched the outside of the far wall relentlessly. Nothing seemed to be out of order. Nothing stolen, thank goodness. He walked through the room and flipped on the switch for the outside. Tiny flakes of sleet blew sideways, sparkling in the glow of the bulb.

A group of ranch horses huddled under the shed, looking at him with troubled eyes. Their breath curled like gray smoke around their noses. His newest horse, Phoenix, held a small black bucket in his mouth as if to say, "See this. It's empty!"

The horses had tramped down the snow until it was hard-packed from their milling and pacing. Since they had not headed out to shelter under the chinaberry groves in the pasture, Lank got the sneaking suspicion they had not been fed. What had Carli been doing all week? Obviously not tending to her ranch.

Lank dipped a half-bucket of oats from the barrel and the horses pushed and shoved, some nipping at each other, like they hadn't seen food in weeks. He suddenly stopped and spun around on his heels. Where was Beau? He ran back inside and sure enough, his headstall, saddle, and blanket were missing. Of all the dumb ideas. That girl didn't have a lick of sense. Going riding in a snowstorm? What was she thinking?

He ran back across the courtyard towards Carli's house. Sharp and cold ice pelted his face. He pulled his coat closer, took a leap over the steps, and landed at the front door to pound on it with both fists. No answer. The house was dark. He tried the knob. Of course, it was unlocked too. Letting himself in and then blindly feeling around for the entry hall switch, he yelled, "Carli!"

No answer. The silence stark and disturbing.

From there he made his way through the house flipping switches as he went. He noticed an old blanket on the living room floor with what looked like small tufts of black hair. What in the world? On the kitchen bar he found her purse and next to that were truck keys and cell phone, plugged in to the wall outlet. She never went anywhere without her phone, and how many times had they all told her to not ride alone? She was such a stubborn, independent girl. It really annoyed him. His mind worked out what to do next. Thinking the impossible but coming to the only logical conclusion.

Carli and Beau had been caught out in this norther. For how long and where, he had no idea. Disregarding the house, which was now lit up like a Christmas tree, he hurried back to the cookhouse punching the sheriff's number on his phone as he ran.

"This is Lank at the Wild Cow."

"It's after midnight," was the gruff reply. "Did Carli make you call me, because she knows I wouldn't answer if it was her." His mumbling soon turned into irritation. "What do you want?"

"She's missing."

"Who's missing?"

"Carli and Beau."

"They're gone? Are you sure?"

"Yes, sir. I think they may be out in this storm."

"Why didn't you say so?" Sheriff Anderson's voice came awake. "I'll initiate the call list and round up some guys to start searching. We'll be at your place in fifteen minutes and then we'll make a plan. If she has a good coat and has found shelter, she might last until morning, but we can't be sure. What's the low for tonight?"

Lank punched his weather app. "Ten degrees." His stomach churned the minute he said it.

The line went dead. Lank hurried back to his house and put on as many layers as he could and still be able to maneuver on a horse. The last thing he grabbed was a silky, royal blue wild rag, a gift from his mother. He wrapped it tightly around his neck, tucking the ends into his shirt front.

He couldn't help but think about how many times Carli had passed through his mind, and how many times he had tried to call her. Is that what his mother had always talked about? The Holy Spirit can work through you and use you. "Watch over us, Mom, and put in a good word with God. Please let Carli be alive." He whispered, trying to hold onto hope as he realized just how much she meant to him.

Chapter Thirty-One

Friday Evening, Ranch Cookhouse

Lank halted at the cookhouse when the door refused to budge. "Good grief." The one door that
was actually locked. He sprinted as fast as he could
against the wind back to his house to find his keys.
They'd need coffee and a plan.

His first instinct was to saddle up and ride out,
but in which direction? He had no idea where Carli
and Beau had gone, and no way of knowing how
long they'd been out there. That's what made his
heart race. He wanted to tear across the pasture
and scream her name, hoping she'd hear above the
wind.

He thought about calling Buck but hesitated.
Knowing his boss, he'd wake Lola and they'd be on
the road within minutes. Lank knew firsthand that
driving in this mess was not safe for anyone, and he
didn't want to risk their lives. After the coffee was
put together, he rummaged through the pantry and

came up empty-handed. He didn't know how long they'd be out in the weather, but the men would need something to warm them up and jolt them awake.

"Thank you, Lola," he said aloud at the discovery of a glass canister of homemade oatmeal cookies. He set those next to the coffee urn and then hurried back outside to saddle his horse.

Instead of fifteen minutes it was more like ten, when he heard the sound of an engine and the slam of vehicle doors. Lank had just poured a cup of coffee and raised his cup for a sip when Nathan Olsen and his little brother, Travis, tumbled through the door.

"Carli's missing?" Nathan took long strides towards him. "For how long?"

"I don't know. When I got here, she and her horse were both gone." Lank paced to the window, looked for more vehicle lights, and paced back to Nathan and his brother.

A blast of cold air made them turn to see Sheriff Anderson leading a group of deputies. He walked with determined steps over to the largest dining table and rolled out paper. They all gathered around a topographic map of the county as he marked the location of Wild Cow Ranch headquarters with a penciled X.

Russell with B&R Beanery came in with a few more men and a large white box. Lank recognized many of the same faces that had risked life and limb to fight their hay barn fire. "Belinda thought we needed banana muffins." The men descended on the box just barely before Russell could set it down. Several men held a muffin in one hand and a cookie in the other, as they all crowded around Sheriff Anderson's map.

"Lank. Tell us what you know."

Before he could answer, the door swung wide again and with that blast of cold all heads turned. The entrance filled with a solid mass of a body as wide and tall as the door frame covered in an ancient buffalo coat. A furry ushanka, Russian ear-flap hat, covered the head and most of the face.

"Vera!" Sheriff Anderson smiled. "I forgot you're on our community emergency call list. Thanks for coming. I hope you have that bloodhound with you."

"Yep, I brought Snot." With that introduction, a dog the size of a yearling cow appeared from behind his owner and stepped into the dining hall. Head erect, with intelligent eyes, he scanned the room, tail wagging so fast it made his entire body wiggle. "He's as harmless as a pet rabbit which makes him a worthless guard dog, but he can follow a scent trail like nobody's business."

"Glad to have you both, Vera." The sheriff set his mouth in a grim line and looked at Lank. "What time did you discover her missing?"

"I noticed all the lights were off when I got here just after dark. Beau and his saddle were gone, and I found Carli's keys, purse, and cell phone at her house."

"She had to have left mid-afternoon I'm assuming. What time did this norther blow in?"

Russell stepped forward. "It started about the time we locked up the coffee shop. I'd say just after four-thirty."

"The worst kicked up around six, maybe seven

o'clock. I was trying to see the interstate about then. Visibility was zero," Lank offered.

"She's been out there in the worst part of it for at least six hours, maybe longer. It's close to midnight now. Where does she usually ride?" the sheriff asked.

"She's trying to learn the ranch and has been taking off in different directions each time. She takes Beau through the heifers on occasion, trying to get him used to cows."

"Okay, that's a good place to start. Where are the heifers?" Sheriff Anderson flattened his hands across the table.

Lank tapped a finger on the map. "Here. And then this road takes you to the North Pasture." Vera walked up behind him. The odor of her coat reminded him of a musty, dirt cellar with the tinge of something dead. No telling how old it was.

"Everybody has 4-wheel drive I'm assuming, because you'll need it. Now think about low places where she might have hunkered down. Are there any barns or structures she could get in for shelter?"

"Several. There's a gas field gathering station here in this area. It has a shed." Lank paused as he studied the map. "I can't think of anything else."

"Russell, you take a few men and follow the county road towards the gathering station. Lank, you drive through the middle of the heifers, and I'll send a couple guys around the perimeter of that pasture. The rest of you, divide up until we have every sector covered." The sheriff made assignments. "Text me every ten minutes or whenever you can get service and let me know your location."

"My horse is saddled," Lank said.

The sheriff looked at him. "Are you sure? You'll get turned around in this mess. I don't have enough men to send out a second search party for you too."

"We'll be fine. I can find the way."

"Snot will go with him. And he can bring them all back," Vera said matter-of-factly.

Lank couldn't think of a nice way to tell Vera to keep her dang dog out of his way, so he just nodded his thanks. Vera nodded back, her forehead creased in a deep frown. In the porch light he could see unshed tears in her eyes. Had Vera even met Carli? Lank didn't have time to think about that now.

"Dress warm then," Sheriff Anderson called after him. "Text me your location. And, Lank, take food and water. She'll be hungry and thirsty. She may be in shock."

The men shuffled out, buttoning coats and pulling on gloves. Lank backtracked to grab a bottle of water and wrapped two muffins in a paper towel. He hurried to where his horse was waiting. Vera and Snot stayed hot on his heels.

"I need somethin' of Carli's."

"What?" Lank was busy checking his saddle, tightening the girth. Phoenix snorted with frustration, knowing he had a job to do, or maybe aggravated at having to go out in the cold.

"Do you have somethin' of hers so Snot can get a whiff?"

"Can he track in the snow?"

"Sure can. The snow is porous and damp. It holds scent real well." Vera turned to look at the next pen. "Is this where her horse stayed?"

"Yes." Lank reached in the tack room and yanked Carli's hoodie that hung on the hook just inside the door. "Will this do?"

Vera opened the gate and yanked Snot inside Beau's pen before taking the jacket. "Perfect." She shoved it under Snot's nose. "This is Carli."

She let the dog loose inside the pen. With nose to the ground, he covered the area with precision, sniffing out every corner and every fence rail. Vera pushed Carli's hoodie into his face again. "Find Carli and Beau," she ordered. The dog whimpered, ready to go.

Lank clenched his jaw with impatience and did everything in his power to hold his tongue. He needed to be going and this pandering to a dog was wasting precious time.

Vera swung open the gate. Snot suddenly took off in a flash dragging Vera running behind, a bobbling giant of fur. She called her dog back and secured him at her side. Lank swung a leg over the saddle and followed them.

Vera closed the gate, made Snot sit, and pointed towards the heifers. "They went that way." Face to face with Snot, she commanded, "Find Carli." Another whiff of the hoodie and Vera unlatched the rope from his collar. With baying that pierced the night air, the dog shot off like a rocket.

"Aren't you coming with us?" Lank asked. He wasn't sure if the dog would follow his commands.

"Only thing you gotta do is keep up." Vera gave a wide grin. "He'll do the rest. I'll catch a ride with some of these other yahoos and find you later. And here, you might need this."

Lank took the small flashlight from Vera's gloved hand. Lank smooched to his horse to send it into a lope after the baying bloodhound. Sure enough, he headed straight up the hill towards the pasture where they kept the heifers. Drifts were well up to his horse's belly in some places, but at least the frigid north wind had calmed, and the blowing snow had stopped, which greatly improved visibility. What little moonlight there was, reflected on the crusty, white landscape. Spiny tops of yucca poked through the snow and dead sagebrush dotted the pasture. He imagined every shadowy clump could be Carli and her horse. How would he ever find them?

Phoenix's hooves crunched as he loped along at a good speed. Lank trusted his horse to step carefully, although he also tried to keep them on the road as best as he could see it. The snow had accumulated enough to make everything one smooth, flat surface of white from bar ditch to bar ditch. The beam of the light helped.

That's the thing about the flat, treeless Texas Panhandle. Snow didn't drift down in fluffy flakes to turn everything into a winter wonderland. It came in sideways, bitter and nasty with a wind that cut right through to your soul. Tonight, the wind had finally died, of that he was glad. Lank's nose tingled from the cold, but otherwise he felt comfortable on top of his horse. If Carli had managed to hunker down somewhere with Beau, she might stay warm enough until she could get her bearings and be able to find her way home.

But Lank had heard of cowboys getting lost in a fog or snow, losing all sense of direction. Horses usually knew the way back to their barn, but in the worst conditions even the animals got turned around. Both horse and rider could freeze to death riding for hours in a circle. His heart fluttered at the grisly thought.

As if Snot had a fire lit under him, he suddenly gave a loud howl and shot off in the dark.

"That danged dog," Lank muttered under his breath as he encouraged his horse to hurry. He could see faint tracks to follow Snot and promised himself that he'd give Crazy Vera a big hug when he got back for the use of her Maglite®.

Lank followed the tracks of the gargantuan bloodhound through the Wild Cow Ranch. He peeked at his phone, squinting against the bright light. Not the greatest thing to do because now it would take his eyes time to adjust to the dark again. It had been almost forty-five minutes since he had called the sheriff. If she went riding around mid-afternoon, Carli had been out in this storm for almost ten hours now. The thought tore at his insides.

"God, if you're listening, please guide Snot to Carli. Please give her the strength to hang on." Lank murmured the prayer out loud, not realizing he had spoken the words until his breath hung like a fog in front of his face. He hadn't prayed in a long time. He had stopped when his mother breathed her last breath.

He finally caught up with Snot at a windmill tank, only because the dog was circling and circling. Agitated about something. Lank wondered if he was thirsty.

Snot suddenly stopped, tilted his head back, and let out a long, moaning howl that could raise the dead. He dug into the snow and raised his head, holding something in his mouth. Lank couldn't tell what it was. A rabbit maybe.

"Where to, Snot? Find Carli."

The dog turned his head towards Lank, refusing to take another step.

"Oh, good grief." Lank swung his leg over and jumped to the ground. "Now is not the time to be digging up a snack. Find Carli." He trudged through the snow, removing a glove to fumble for the phone in his shirt pocket. He needed to call Vera and find out how to make the dog stay on the trail. The cold stiffened his once warm fingers and he had trouble turning on the light.

"What'a ya got? Find Carli." He couldn't hide the frustration in his voice. He had half a mind to keep riding and forget about the dang dog.

He decided to shine the beam towards the dog's face. Hurrying closer he reached out a hand to take something from Snot's mouth. He drew a sharp breath. Carli's beanie.

"Good boy." Lank showered the dog with praise and patted his head. "Find Carli."

Snot couldn't contain his excitement. He stood up on his hind legs, did a twirl, and with a loud howl spun around into a run at full tilt. But this time he dashed under the barbed wire and disappeared into the darkness.

Lank couldn't slow the beat of his heart as he looked at the knit hat he held. "Snot! Snot, come back!" That blamed dog. Why would he go into the neighbor's pasture? And then the realization of where he was hit Lank. Right across that fence line was an old barn. Their fence line neighbors used it to store hay, as the structure wasn't good for much else. Could it be that Carli had found some place safe to wait out the storm?

Chapter Thirty-Two

Saturday Morning, Early on Christmas Eve

Cold.
Wind.
Never ceasing wind.

It rattled the barn and whistled through the wide boards. No, this wasn't a barn. There were window screens. And Carli refused to move. She was warm and snuggly under a heavy comforter. She heard him calling her. Lank. Who would name a kid that anyway? Maybe it's short for something like Leroy. Lawrence? Lancaster? Or a nickname because he was a lanky kid? But he was anything but lanky. He was compact and muscular, with not an ounce of fat on him anywhere. Dark hair and neatly trimmed facial hair with a grin that made her knees go weak, and that coppery brown skin that surrounded those gray-blue eyes. Eyes she could get lost in. The windows were gone now and from her bed Carli could see endless green pastures dotted with black calves, running and tumbling into each other.

The green suddenly turned to wood. Bright chandeliers hung overhead, and the sunlight reflected through ornate windows. Buck stood at the altar of the sanctuary holding a Bible. "Carli, Christmas is a beautiful time of remembrance. A time to celebrate when Jesus came to the earth as a baby. He came for us, you know. He became human so He could feel all of our pain and heartache and loneliness. He loves you like a daughter. He's your true Father. You have a family."

Carli's vision blurred and she saw a fuzzy, dim light descending from the altar, arms outstretched as if welcoming her home. Carli could feel His love. She felt a peace cover her like a warm blanket. It was good. She didn't want to leave the warmth. Was this Heaven?

She walked towards Buck, noticing that she wore a white, billowing dress that rustled on the wooden floors.

"Carlotta Jean Jameson. Lancaster Michael Torres." Buck smiled at them.

Lank stepped closer and wrapped his arms around her. Then he kissed her lips, her cheeks, her nose, her eyes, her neck. Slobbery. Wet. Cold.

She brushed her face with her sleeve. Too much spit. And then she woke with a start.

Carli's jaw trembled. She couldn't stop shivering and her heart beat ninety miles a minute. Maybe she had dreamed someone was calling her name but now all she heard was the wind. The old tin moaned and snapped. Surely it would collapse on her at any minute.

And then a howl like nothing she had ever heard before split the night and drowned out the wind. More slobbery kisses.

"Carli." Her name again. Far away, carried over the wind. It was a dream. No one was coming for her. She blinked, remembering where she was but it was dark. She needed to saddle her horse, although Beau didn't know the lay of the land any better than she did. They'd have to take their chances. She couldn't stay here until morning. She shivered again and tried to stand but couldn't, the cold reaching to her core and making her eyes water.

More wet on her face. No. A rough, wet tongue slid over her nose and mouth. This wasn't a dream. This was real. Her goose down jacket had slipped off the top of her head. In the moonlight shadows, Carli stared into the face of a slobbering monster with beady eyes, a black nose covered in snow. The cold, generously wet tongue slid over her eyes this time, the body wiggled from the tail wagging in overdrive. She sat up with a jolt. "Who are you?"

"That would be Snot. He tracked you here."

She blinked in the bright light that shone in her face.

And there he was, suddenly standing in front of her, the light from his cell phone casting a beam on the hay floor and shadows around her storm shelter.

Carli was never so glad to see the most annoying cowboy she had ever known in her life. He walked closer. His face in the shadows. Those dreamy eyes, dark complexion overcast with several days of scruffy beard. Her heart skipped a beat.

He stood near her horse, one arm resting on

Beau's back end.

His name was the only thing she could manage to utter. "Lank?" Or was he a mirage, still part of the dream?

"Can you stand up?" He turned his attention away from her for a moment to look over her horse. "Beau looks solid. He doesn't seem to be too upset."

She blinked. "Home is not a place."

"Carli. You're in a barn." Lank walked closer tugging Snot out of her face. "Settle down, Snot. I thought hound dogs liked to sleep a lot."

"Ho-o-ome." Her teeth chattered. She didn't know why standing made her feel the norther storm to her very core. "Not just a p-p-place."

"We'll be there in a minute. Carli. Wake up." He snapped his fingers in her face. "Can you ride? Do you need a doctor?"

Carli suddenly sprang to her feet and ran into his arms, almost knocking him over. She wrapped both arms around him and squeezed as tight as she could. He felt real. Solid bone and muscle. This wasn't a dream.

The thought of getting back on her horse made her shiver. She really hated the notion of riding out in that snow all the way back to ranch headquarters. She didn't answer, instead looked from Beau to the outside and back to her horse. She stared at Lank but couldn't say anything. The snow had finally stopped but the wind moaned a sad song. The moon's glow cast a faint blue light over the white landscape.

Lank untangled himself from Carli's arms and punched his phone. "Sheriff. I found her. Yeah, she's okay. Just about near frozen is all. A little disoriented. Can you bring a trailer around? I don't think she wants to ride. We're across the fence line in the old Ackerman barn."

Carli swallowed and rubbed the sleep from her eyes. She willed herself to wake up. "What time is it?" Carli finally managed to mutter.

"Well after midnight. How long have you been here?"

"It's hard to say. I forgot my phone and lost track of time. The day was so beautiful, I just kept riding and riding. Not very smart in the middle of winter, I guess."

"Haven't you ever heard the saying, if you can wear flipflops and snow boots in the same day, you must live in the Texas Panhandle? Northers can blow across here and come out of nowhere. When I couldn't find you or Beau at headquarters, I knew something was up. Thank goodness you left that gate open."

"I know, it's a major sin in this country, but I wasn't sure if the gate led into another pasture on the Wild Cow or into a neighbor's place."

"Oh, I almost forgot." Lank walked over to his horse that was loosely tied at the opening to the barn. Phoenix wasn't going anywhere in this storm. Lank dug around in the saddle bag. "Sheriff said you'd need this." He handed her a muffin and bottle of water. It took most of her strength to tear the muffin in half without having the monster-sized dog scrambling into her lap.

Carli sat back down on the hay bale and then laughed. Snot followed. "Here ya go. My hero." She held out a piece of muffin to the dog and glanced up at Lank. He frowned. The look of irritation on his face made her laugh again. She bent down and kissed the dog on the forehead.

"Why didn't you let Beau bring you back? You were only about five miles from headquarters. But it's hard to say when a norther that bad blows in."

So much for the niceties. "How about, 'Good to see you, Carli. Glad you're not a popsicle, Carli.' Just moving right into the chewing me out part, are you?"

Carli glared at her rescuer. She didn't know whether to hug him again or smack him across the face.

Chapter Thirty-Three

"What were you thinking?" Lank stood with his feet apart and hands on his hips, giving Carli a look of pure aggravation. His face looked mean in the shadows, from behind the beam of light cast by his cell phone that made her eyes squint. They glared at each other. The snow and wind had stopped. Behind him hung the heavy darkness of night. She couldn't see anything past the opening of the old barn.

Carli let out a sigh, her breath hanging in the air. Why would a cowboy ride all this way through the snow only to rescue his boss and then scold her like she was a toddler? Carli was too tired and cold to explain herself. She felt like a limp noodle.

"On second thought, Beau might have gotten turned around in the storm. Y'all could have been wandering all night. Why did you even leave your house this morning?"

Would he ever stop with the questions? "It wasn't morning. I told you already. It happened to be a beautiful sunny afternoon." The sudden heart swooning feelings she had felt for Lank when she first saw him standing in the frigid barn had vanished. She hung her head. "If I'm that much of a pain, why are you even here?"

Her stomach growled but she couldn't take another bite. Nothing better than Belinda's muffins. Snot was more than willing to help. What she needed was a huge mug of hot coffee to go with it. She looked at Lank. "And yes, I should have headed straight back to headquarters at the first snowflake. But it changed so fast. I panicked. The sleet turned to snow and then I couldn't see my hand in front of me. My ears were about frozen off after I lost my cap."

"This cap?" He pulled it from his back pocket.

"Where'd you find it?" She used both hands to pull it on. Her head and ears felt so cozy now. She sighed and sank down on the pile of hay bales.

"Actually, Snot found it. By a windmill."

"That's right, when I stopped to fill up my canteen." Carli leaned down to shower kisses on top of Snot's head. "Good boy. Such a smart boy."

Lank plopped onto the hay bale next to Carli, opened the water bottle she was struggling with, and handed it back to her. "Drink."

Carli took a long draw. The silence grew awkward between them as she drank. He watched her intently. She could feel his stare.

"I'm glad you're okay," he finally muttered. He spoke so softly she might not have heard him if they hadn't been sitting so close together.

"What? You're not going to gripe at me anymore?" She took another long gulp of water.

"Sorry about that. You had me so worried when I got home and found you gone."

"Did you have fun at your sister's?"

"For the most part." He suddenly grew silent and glum.

"I am really glad to see you." She couldn't help herself. She leaned closer and gave him another hug.

"I thought we had to keep this on a professional level. You know, employee-employer."

"It is after midnight and officially Christmas Eve so I make exceptions on holidays." They both laughed.

Guilt washed over Carli as she remembered the last time they talked, and she made that snide remark about Christmas. And even after that he still rode through a foot of snow to find her. "About what I said just before you left, I'm sorry. I didn't realize this was the first Christmas without your mother. I should have been more sensitive."

"Why do you hate Christmas so much?"

"Just recently, I've had a lot of time to think about that." She laughed. "It's amazing what being snowed in can do for your soul searching."

"Yeah, I've done some thinking too." His eyes almost twinkled.

"I guess the reason I ignored the holiday is because the commercialization is so overrated. My house in Georgia was very minimal. I didn't decorate at all. My business partner, Mark, always invited me to join his family but I never went." Carli had worked with the man for many years but knew nothing about his family. She remained guarded, both professionally and personally.

"That's a lie." Lank said matter-of-factly and without apology.

"I just poured out my heart and soul and you're calling me a liar?"

"Are you telling me that a bunch of Christmas trees and tinsel are what gets you all stressed out? What a crock. Tell me the real reason."

Carli delayed her response by drinking deeply from the plastic bottle. She knew the answer and with every fiber of her being hated to blurt it out. Stating something out loud made it a fact, and you couldn't retrieve it once it was out there. She didn't want to tell anyone her innermost thoughts and most particularly to some Texas cowpuncher. She hated talking about her feelings. What a waste of energy.

"Well? We have a wait until they can get the trailer hitched and pull it through the pasture in this snow. If the pickup truck doesn't work, they may have to use the tractor. So, you're stuck here with me for a while, unless you want to jump on your horse and take your chances on the open range again."

He was the most annoying person she knew. Carli frowned and swallowed the lump in her throat. "Christmas always reminds me..."

"Go on."

She took a deep breath. "This time of year reminds me how alone I really am. If I ignore it, I don't have to be reminded. There, I said it. Are you happy now?" Tears stung her eyes, and it was everything she could do not to start sobbing. Plus, she was freezing and tired. That didn't help the situation.

"That's what I thought." Lank put his arm around her. "Don't you feel better just saying it?"

Carli rubbed her runny nose with the sleeve of her goose down jacket. "How'd you know?"

"I saw you bristle when we walked into the cookhouse last Saturday for lunch. You were as jumpy as a long-tailed cat in a room full of rocking chairs. Then I got to thinking how much I dreaded Christmas this year. It used to be my favorite holiday. But not this year and I knew why. It just made sense because you never had any family really, except for your foster parents. And I was missing my mother so I guess I could relate to being an orphan, so to speak."

"And then I made a horrible remark about hating Christmas and there you were without your mom this year. I'm sorry." Carli wiped her face again and turned to look at him. His warm breath caressed her cheek. His blue-gray eyes softened when he looked at her. Carli couldn't help but panic. If he leaned closer to lay a kiss on her lips, she'd have to fire him.

He tapped her nose with a gloved hand. "Not getting close to anyone makes for a dull existence though. It might feel safer that way, but it's no way to live."

Carli gasped. He nailed the very core of her. She rarely let anyone get this close. "How could you possibly know that?"

"I know when you're sad, when you're happy, when you're stressed. Like how much you hate the song Here Comes Santa Claus." He chuckled.

"I pretty much know everything there is to know about you, Carli Jameson."

She wanted him to lean closer, even if her lips were blue from the cold. Good grief, she must look a fright, but she saw acceptance and kindness in his eyes. There was something deeper there too, but it scared her, and she wasn't ready. She broke their eye contact.

"Thanks, Lank. I guess I owe you. You want a raise or something?" She giggled.

"I'd settle for a few of those kisses you planted on Snot's head." His lips crushed hers so fast it took her breath away. Cold and warm at the same time, she felt that kiss all the way to her toes. At that moment, she didn't want anything more in her life than to be here with him.

The darkness was suddenly pierced by lights, and they heard the steady chug of an engine.

He pulled away, cussed softly. "They brought the tractor." Lank jumped up and ran outside.

Within seconds a group swarmed into the barn. Sheriff Anderson followed by Crazy Vera and the fire chief, all talking at once, suddenly bulged into the barn. Carli had never been so happy to see a group of people. She jumped up and ran towards them.

"Good Lord, girl. We've been worried sick about you!" Miss Vera stepped forward looking like a wet Sasquatch. She wrapped Carli in a bear hug. It literally felt like she was hugging a bear. That coat had a strange smell. Vera pulled back from the hug and wrapped a scratchy, woolen blanket around Carli's shoulders.

The others gathered around Carli, patting and

hugging. Petting Beau.

Vera's voice rang out over the hubbub. "Snot!"

The big bloodhound came lumbering up out of the darkness, snow covering his muzzle. His tail wagging like a whirligig in someone's summer yard. He bounded to his mistress where he was rewarded with a pat on the head. Then he sat on Carli's boot and licked her hand.

"Yes, I know you found her. Good job, fella." Vera grabbed his head between her hands and scratched both ears at the same time.

Chief Mack stepped closer to Carli. "Are you okay?" He clicked a tiny penlight and shined it in both her eyes, looking at her face intently.

"Yes, I'm fine."

"She's probably dehydrated but no signs of shock. I think she's going to be all right once she warms up." Chief Mack nodded to the sheriff.

"Good then. Let's get going." Sheriff Anderson took charge of the scene and had everybody moving towards the trailer.

Chief Mack untied Beau and Lank got Phoenix. The horses were loaded into the trailer. "One more cold ride and then we'll get you warm and toasty." Sheriff Anderson patted Carli on the shoulder.

Surprisingly it was Vera who climbed up on the tractor. "Load up!" Despite the fact the sheriff had already given the order, Vera's voice boomed into the dark night. Lank shut the middle gate in the trailer behind the horses and the rest of them piled in the back.

"Hang on a minute, Vera." Lank ran back to the barn and returned with a square bale, which he busted and spread over the wooden slates of the trailer floor. They all sat. Snot plopped down in the middle.

It was a slow and bumpy ride across the pasture and through the snow. Carli could barely keep her eyes open. She leaned against Lank's shoulder and muttered, "What is your full name?" The dream appeared clear in her mind. "Is your first name Lancaster, Lank for short?"

"No. Why?" he whispered back.

"No reason. Just wondering." Carli closed her eyes and looped her arm with his. There was no way in heck she'd ever tell anyone about that dream.

Chapter Thirty-Four

Saturday Morning, Around 2:00 AM, Christmas Eve Day

Carli woke with a start from a bump to her head. The livestock trailer lurched again as they bounced over the snowy pasture towards home. She fought to sit up straight without leaning on Lank. Home. She smiled without opening her eyes.

It was hard to believe the nightmare she had experienced only a few hours before. It could have turned out a lot worse. Thank God, it hadn't. As they topped the hill, she looked through the trailer slats. In the distance outside floodlights formed soft pools of light on the white snow around the two-story cookhouse. She had never been happier to see a place before.

Home.

"We've got a lot to do," she muttered to no one in particular.

"There's nothing you have to do right now." Lank

heard her. "You need a hot shower, food, and sleep."

"I can sleep next year." Her voice rang out over the silent pasture as they got closer to headquarters.

The tractor pulled to a stop, and someone unlatched the trailer gate.

Vera's voice boomed in the dark. "Let's get her inside and warmed up." At the sound of his mistress's voice, Snot shot up with a tail wag, licked Carli's face one last time, and bounded out of the trailer.

"There's my boy. Good boy." Crazy Vera showered him with kisses and belly rubs. "I'm goin' to cook you a roast dinner fit for a king. Yes, I am." If dogs could smile, that's how his face looked.

Lank tapped her shoulder. "Carli. We're home. Come talk to everyone first. They were sure worried about you."

He offered a hand and tugged her to stand. Every joint and bone in her body seemed to ache. She glanced through the gate behind her in the front of the trailer and saw that Beau was fine.

"Don't worry about him. I'll get him settled." Lank nudged her towards the back end of the trailer. She stepped down into a big bear hug from Vera.

"I was crazy with worry, girl, but I was prayin' too. So glad you're home," Vera said.

Behind them gathered a group of people. Belinda stepped out in front and wrapped her in a hug. Lights from pickup trucks and Jeeps glistened on the snowy ground. Several vehicles were parked around the cookhouse, covered in snow. Men piled out, dressed in heavy canvas coats, gloves, woolen caps, their identities hidden behind wild rags or face wraps blocking out the cold. They looked like they belonged in Alaska instead of the Texas Pan-handle.

Carli grinned through misty eyes.

Home.

Home is more than a place. Home is a feeling. Home is with the people who love you.

The neighbors walked towards her, calling out greetings followed by pats on her shoulder and more hugs.

"You all leave her alone and let her get inside," boomed Vera. She squeezed her bulk through the crowd and grabbed Carli by the arm none too gently. "Come with me." With no option but to follow, they headed across the churned-up snow towards the cookhouse. Carli's cheeks stung when she stepped inside the warmth.

Belinda placed a steaming mug of coffee in her hand. The smell of the coffee was a preview of the warmth to come, clear to her toes. She sniffed deeply and took a sip. The warm liquid slid down her throat and hit her empty belly.

"Whoa. What is that?"

"A special family remedy for aches and pain. Just drink it. My grandmother used to call it her hot toddy." Belinda gently pushed the mug back towards Carli's lips.

For the next half hour Carli said thank you about a gazillion times and Lank repeated the story of Snot's heroic efforts. She had to listen to a few snow stories from every cowboy there, and she loved every one of them.

Finally, Lank raised his hands and whistled. The voices quieted. "On behalf of the Wild Cow Ranch I just want to thank everyone again for your help in finding our boss. We're thankful she's back and wasn't hurt. Her horse, too. Thank God for sending us some help. Sheriff, we really appreciate all that you and your men did."

Sheriff Anderson stepped to the front of the crowd. He draped an arm around Carli's shoulders. "Thanks, guys, for answering the call so promptly." He turned to Carli. "I'm glad you're okay and I want to publicly apologize for this week. I lost my temper several times and I'm sorry."

Carli laughed as the others looked on with perplexed expressions. "You had every right to get perturbed with me. I lost count of how many times I called you this week."

Sheriff Anderson and Carli exchanged glances and then both laughed.

She fought to keep her voice strong and her eyes dry. "I want to thank everyone too. And I want to thank you for the welcome you all extended to me when I moved to this community. This is home. I realize that now. Which is why I'd like to revive the annual tradition started by my Grandmother Jean. Next year I hope you'll join us at the Wild Cow for Christmas cookies and a holiday light show that will be out of this world. Bring your families."

"What light show?" Lank asked.

More hugs and Merry Christmas cheers were exchanged as everyone piled on their winter gear and headed back home. Carli felt bone tired, but she was wired too and didn't know if she could sleep after all that had happened this night. Might also be due to the mug of Belinda's special coffee and two muffins she just ate.

"Why don't y'all come to my house tonight for

Christmas Eve dinner?" Carli turned to Lank. "Will you text Buck and Lola and tell them to be there?"

He nodded.

"Okay, great. And Lank, I need your help with something else."

They picked up trash and put coffee cups in the sink, then turned off lights in the kitchen and dining hall. Lank followed Carli outside.

"Where to, boss?"

"Are the horses doing okay?"

"They're both settled in and doing fine."

"Follow me then."

"You're the boss." Lank yawned but didn't argue and fell into step beside her.

Chapter Thirty-Five

Saturday Morning, Early, Christmas Eve Day

Carli led Lank Torres to her house. Since he was the ranch hand, he might as well help with her crazy scheme. They would have to hurry to finish by Christmas Eve dinner, which was only ten or so hours away.

They took off their coats and boots, leaving everything in the entry hall by the front door. In stocking feet, she led him through the kitchen. "I need all the boxes from the basement labeled 'Christmas' brought up here. I'll put on some coffee first."

Lank stepped closer, blocking her path to the coffee pot. "I realize you don't like Christmas, but that's no reason to throw out all of your grandparents' stuff. Slow down. Do we have to do this right now? Think about what you're doing." Concern filled his eyes. A frown etched his forehead. If he wasn't so darn cute, she would have boxed his ears.

"I'm not throwing anything away. We're decorating."

Lank looked at her with a dumbfounded expression. Shoot, that was cute too.

"Now hurry. I want everything done before Lola and Buck get back. And then we'll go to church, and afterwards eat a huge Christmas Eve dinner here at my house. It's what Jean and Ward would want. It's what I want."

"Alrighty then," Lank mumbled as he watched her intently. He still didn't let her get by to make coffee, but he took a step back. "Are you okay?"

"Just because they're not here doesn't mean their house, my house, can't be as lively as it once was. Let's invite everyone we know." Carli dodged around him.

Moments later the door to the basement squeaked as she opened it. Rough wooden board steps led down into darkness. She leaned forward and felt along the wall. "I can never remember where the light switch is."

"What are we doing?"

"I need your help carrying some boxes up. Haven't you been listening?" The switch clicked and Carli stepped carefully down.

"Boxes? It's almost five in the morning, Carli. Can't this wait till tomorrow?"

"Christmas decorations."

"Oh, jeez," he muttered, which was all the complaint he had as he followed her into the musty basement.

Against a back wall, containers were stacked, all neatly labeled. Red Christmas balls, tinsel, breakable ornament, lights.

"Which ones do you need?" Lank asked as he reached for the top row and grabbed a box marked Red Bows.

"All of them."

He froze, holding the box in mid-air over his head. "All of them?"

"Yes, and I need you to help me decorate the house too. We don't have much time before it'll be Christmas Eve dinner and Buck and Lola will be here."

He set the box on the floor and turned to look at her like she was crazy, his face reflecting the weariness of no sleep and hours of riding in the cold.

Carli turned to face him. "Thanks again, Lank. I really appreciate that you came looking for me." She studied his face. Her stomach fluttered. She wanted more than anything to reach out and touch that face. To kiss him and tell him that for the first time in her life she felt safe and not alone. There were so many times in her life she had felt scared and unsure. Wondering where she should go. Realizing no one cared. But now she finally understood what home meant.

"And I need your help with one more thing. I really want to decorate for Christmas. Will you help me?"

For a split second she got the feeling that he was going to kiss her, but he ducked his head and picked up the box of bows. "Whatever you say, boss."

She followed him upstairs, staring at his back and the muscles that flexed underneath his snug fitting waffle shirt as he balanced the boxes. Her lips still tingled from the kiss they had shared in the barn.

This time if he tried to kiss her again, she wouldn't stop him.

Lank was all business by the time they got the last of the boxes carried up from the basement of her grandparents' house. Carli was running on pure adrenaline from caffeine. Or was it a new-found joy for this time of year? A new beginning? She couldn't tell.

They found an artificial tree in a box. And she tuned to a station that played all Christmas songs. They got to work, sorting branches and figuring out what row came next. When it was all done, the tree filled an entire corner of the living room. They had to move some furniture out of the way. While Lank searched in boxes for ornaments, Carli cooked them a quick breakfast of frozen waffles and bacon before they began unpacking.

"Mmmm, this is good. Thank you." Lank dug in to his food without even glancing her way. She couldn't help but wish for that moment again in the dark basement. She wanted to ask him if he had wanted to kiss her. They should explore this attraction that hovered over them like a gray cloud, but she was scared. With a quiet sigh and a heavy heart, she refilled their coffee cups.

"Why are you back anyway?" Carli returned to the table. "I thought you were staying at your sister's for the holiday?"

He hesitated for a moment, as if choosing his words and thinking about what he wanted to say. She wished he felt more comfortable around her.

"She wants to go through Mom's stuff and asked me to help." He hesitated. "I tried, but I can't stay in my mom's house for very long."

Carli realized how hard it had been for Lank to admit his sadness. "I'm glad you came back early." She laid an arm on his shoulder. "I can never thank you enough."

"We have lots to do so we may as well get back at it." Lank stood, hurriedly changing the subject and carried his plate to the sink before disappearing around the corner into the living room.

After Carli said it, she worried that her reply seemed empty and heartless. She hadn't expressed much sympathy for his loss or having to deal with his mom's belongings. Carli couldn't even imagine what that was like. She had plenty of other people's possessions but hadn't known the people it had all belonged to.

They unwrapped more ornaments and found sacks of garland. Tinsel went around the tree and across every window. The mantel became a base for every holiday candle she found. Some with charcoal-colored wicks and some brand new still in cellophane wrapping, in every size and color. One box held holiday serving pieces and the gaudiest tablecloth she had ever seen. Green checks with bright red poinsettias, trimmed with stiff cranberry-colored lace. She decided to complete the table setting with felt Santa Claus face placemats and crisp white cloth napkins she found in a drawer. Her grandmother's Christmas dishes were red and white with scenes of sleighs and horses. The backs of the plates were stamped Currier & Ives, which she recognized. Carli had never seen china that pretty. Her heart swelled. It was hers now.

She hung greenery on the wagon wheel chandelier and twinkling lights around the gilt-framed mirror. The dining room dressed up nice, and she smiled at her handiwork. While she carefully placed dishes and silverware on the table, Lank started a fire in the fireplace and then collapsed on the sofa. Carli sank down beside him, admiring the crackling fire. The tree reached to the ceiling and not one bough was left untouched. No telling how many ornaments they had unboxed. The topper was a glittery Texas star. She wondered about the people who had gathered in this very room years before, without her. She could never go back though. She was here now and that's all that mattered.

"It looks good." Carli stifled a yawn.

"Yes, it does."

"Thanks for your help."

"Anytime, boss." He laid his hand on her leg and she rested her head on his shoulder. She just needed to close her eyes for a minute.

"Knock, knock! Anyone home?"

Carli's eyes fluttered as she covered her mouth with a hand and stretched her arms over her head. She opened her eyes to see Buck and Lola in her living room along with a girl standing behind them who looked a lot like Lola but a foot taller.

She blinked and then remembered Lank's hand was still on her thigh, but she sat frozen, trying to remember where she was. She should stand up. This doesn't look good.

"What are y'all doing here?" Carli blinked and rubbed the sleep from her eyes.

"We got Lank's text with an invitation for Christmas Eve dinner. Did you forget?"

"We've been busy."

Buck's eyebrows raised. Lola had a deep frown etched on her face, her eyes stony with anger.

Chapter Thirty-Six

Carli leaned squished against Lank on her couch and stared up at the people who stood in her living room. Yes, Lank had spent the night at her house but it wasn't what it looked like. After an awkward moment of silence that stretched out too long, Carli realized Lank was not going to say anything that might help them out of this jam.

"We've been busy decorating," Carli said uneasily, an unwelcome blush across her warm cheeks. "Been putting up stuff all night. Actually, since early morning I guess it was. He helped. We must've fallen asleep." She glanced at Lank. "How long have we been out?"

A lazy grin spread across his face but he didn't offer any further explanation. Carli shot him an irritated glare and then stood up to face the inquisition. She worried that Buck and Lola might think less of her.

Amusement shone in Buck's eyes as he cleared his throat.

"It's all my fault," Lola said, a deep frown of concern showing on her face. She hugged Carli tight and didn't let go when Carli tried to pull away. Finally, she stepped back and put her hands on Carli's shoulders. "I was the one who insisted we leave town and then you got lost and almost froze yourself to death. Can you ever forgive me?" Tears welled within her eyes.

"That's what you're upset about?" Carli hugged her again. "I got myself in this pickle, and I would have done the same whether you and Buck had been at home or not. Lank found me. I'm okay."

"The sheriff called me late last night and filled me in on the details. We left early this morning and got back as soon as we could," Buck added.

"Oh, I forgot." Lola turned and tugged on the arm of the girl that stood behind her. "This is our niece, Rena. I am so happy for you to meet each other. Rena came back with us. Carli is not frozen. My Christmas Eve is now complete. My two girls are both here." Lola beamed at them, joy shining in her eyes. She wiped one cheek with the back of her hand and sniffed.

Carli stared at Rena for a minute, unsure what to say. Her brain was still fuzzy from lack of sleep.

"I've always wanted a sister," said Rena. "Nice meeting you."

Carli laughed. "Me, too." A sense of relief washed over her. Maybe the Lank incident was behind them and already forgotten.

Buck pushed back his cowboy hat and hooked his thumbs in his jean pockets as he stopped at the doorway and looked from side to side. "Never thought I'd see the day when somebody could outdo my Lola on decorations."

"I must say, y'all sure went all out." Lola walked around the room stopping in front of the fireplace mantel before moving over to the tree. "You must have emptied every box in storage. I haven't seen some of these ornaments in years and years."

She pulled a horse off the branch and held it up by the satin ribbon. The pink iridescent color of its body and the flowing mane of silky purple glittered in the blinking lights. "I remember this ornament. Jean bought it at the National Finals Rodeo one year. She had planned to give it to you. She was always buying things for you. She'd say, 'Carlotta will love this.'" Lola didn't look at Carli as she talked. She held the horse carefully as though it was the most precious treasure in the world, and then she carefully placed it back on the tree.

Carli wondered how many more things in this house had been bought with her in mind.

"And that tablecloth." Lola laughed. "Do you remember it, Buck? Jean hated that tablecloth. It was a gift from her father-in-law's spinster sister. But being Jean, she got it out every year just in case the old woman ever showed up for Christmas dinner." Lola ran her hand over the fabric and looked around the room. "You did good here, Carli. Lank, you, too. Jean and Ward would have been so thrilled."

Carli didn't know what to say, other than she was more determined than ever to continue the legacy her grandparents had left her.

"I hope you're hungry. Everybody, help me bring in the food." Lola turned and headed for the front door.

"What time is it? I need to put a ham in the oven." Carli straightened her wrinkled shirt. She probably should take a shower and change before dinner.

Lola laughed. "It's almost seven o'clock. Since I didn't hear from you all afternoon, I figured you were dead to the world after your snow adventure. I cooked everything and then we went to church early for Christmas Eve services." She glanced around the room. "Oh look, Buck. Carli already has the table set and it's so pretty."

"Do I have time for a shower?" Carli asked.

"Food's ready," said Lola as she walked out the front door.

"Let's eat then," answered Buck, following her.

Buck, Lola, Rena, and Lank brought in dish after dish and set everything out on the table. Lola stepped back several times to survey the spread, rearranging things here and there.

"Just a sec. I forgot something." Carli found a lighter wand in the kitchen drawer and lit every candle on the fireplace mantel and on the dining room table. Just as she had ice in the glasses and the sweet tea poured, a knock on the door surprised her. But before she could answer it, Lank said, "They made it." He rushed into the entry hall, and she heard greetings and hellos and laughter.

"I invited my sister. Hope that's okay." Lank appeared in the doorway with a woman, a man, and two boys. "This is my older sister Kelly, her husband Matt, and my two nephews, Zachary and Zane."

At the mention of their names, the two boys forgot their manners and lunged at their Uncle Lank. Carli would have guessed that was his sister without him telling her. They favored each other except that Kelly had dyed her hair blonde, but she had the same blue-gray eyes of her little brother.

Her husband Matt had much darker skin, with a wide-friendly smile and the boys were the perfect combination of both. They huddled in the entry hall.

"Of course, they're welcome, and if I know Lola, there's plenty of food. Come on in." Carli gave them a big smile and pointed towards the dining room.

With her greeting, their faces relaxed, and they filled the living room. Carli offered to take coats, but instead Matt immediately gave her a big bear hug.

"I'm really glad you're here," Lank said to his sister. "I was afraid the roads would be too bad."

"The ranch roads are the only ones still snow packed. The highways are clear. It wouldn't have made any difference. We wanted to be with you tonight." She gave her brother a hug.

Lola, Buck, and Rena said hello along with more hugs; obviously they all knew Lank's family. Someone brought extra chairs from the office, and Carli found more plates for the boys who sat at one end. With enough seats, they all found places at the table. Everyone turned to Carli. She wasn't sure what to do. She had never hosted a Christmas Eve dinner before. In the wrinkled clothes she had been wearing for the past two days, she sat at the head of the table and looked at the people gathered in her home. Everyone looked so clean and shiny, all dressed in their Christmas sweaters except for her and Lank. They both looked like they had spent the night in a barn in the middle of a December norther, which is exactly what they had done. Buck smiled at her and nodded his head.

"Merry Christmas Eve everyone and thanks for

joining me. I have come to realize that home isn't a physical place. Home resides in your heart and in your mind wherever you are. It's a feeling you get from the people around you. Even though I'll never know my birth family who lived here, I want to thank you all for making me feel like family. Buck, will you please say the blessing?"

Heads bowed as Buck's deep Texas drawl blessed the food and the hands that prepared it. A resounding "Amen" from all and then arms reached for bowls that began circulating the table.

Carli couldn't help but feel tears in the back of her eyes. She swallowed the lump in her throat as she looked around the table. No, these people weren't of her blood, but they had come to mean just as much to her. God did have plans for her, and without a doubt she felt certain this was where she was supposed to be. At this time. At this place, with these people.

"Amen and thank you, Lord," she muttered under her breath and then said, "Especially thanks to the hands that prepared it, that being Lola, and not me. But Lank and I do get credit for the decorations." Laughter and smiles filled the dining room as the food continued to be passed.

Lola had brought ham and a turkey with dressing, several kinds of vegetables and of course, her yeast dinner rolls. At first, Carli felt a tinge of guilt for inviting everyone over to her house, and then contributing nothing to the meal but then she bit into a hot, buttery roll and her taste buds rejoiced.

Chapter Thirty-Seven

"I remember these dishes." Kelly held up the red and white bread plate and turned to Carli. "Lank's worked here at the Wild Cow since high school, so your grandmother always included us. She loved these dishes."

"Do you remember where she got them?" asked Carli.

"They were an anniversary present, I think. Is that right, Hon?" Lola looked at Buck.

"Not sure about that, but I do recall Jean wanting Christmas dishes. She left many hints with Ward, and he always grumbled about her not needing any more holiday junk. He knew that he'd be the one to get it out of storage or hang it up." Buck chuckled.

"She used them every year," added Kelly.

"What about the set with the cattle brands around the edges and the Longhorn in the middle?"

"That was her china pattern when she got married," said Lola.

Carli took a quick breath of surprise. Those dishes were antiques and she couldn't help but ask,

"China pattern? What does that mean?"

"Didn't the lady who raised you have a china pattern?" Lola looked at Carli, surprise on her face.

"Every girl in the South has one. Sometimes you pick it out when you're in high school for your hope chest," Kelly said.

Rena grinned and spoke up. "I'm single, and have my China pattern all picked out. I've got pictures and the registry number."

Lola nodded in agreement. "Or sometimes you decide after you're engaged. It's tradition."

"What's to decide?" asked Carli.

"The pattern, the color, the design on your formal set of china. You go to the store and add it to your bridal registry, and then people buy you the pieces as a wedding gift," explained Kelly.

"And then after you're married, the beautiful china goes into the stately china cabinet," Buck interjected.

"But the number one rule," Kelly held up her finger. "It stays in the cabinet. Boys, what does momma say about her wedding china?"

Zachary Matthew swallowed a mouthful of bread. "Never touch the blue dishes."

"That's right," Kelly beamed with pride at her oldest.

"And the other rule is never actually eat off the wedding china. And never be alone in your madness. Convince other newly-engaged brides that they must pick out a pattern that is never to be used or seen," said Matt causing the room to burst into laughter.

"Did we get dishes for our wedding?" asked Buck.

"No, dear. We couldn't afford a big wedding, and

no one offered to give us a shower, remember?" Lola's smile turned to a sadness shadowing her eyes.

Conversation switched to other topics, the weather being one. Carli had to fill Matt and Kelly in about her first Texas norther. Matt told them about growing up in Houston and his first memory of seeing snow. And of course, Buck had more than one snowstorm story to tell.

"Where are the pies?" asked Lola. "They must still be in the car."

"I'll get them," offered Buck.

"I'll make coffee then." Lola stood and took a couple of dirty dishes with her.

After everyone pitched in and carried their plates to the kitchen and the table was cleared, they settled in the living room with coffee and pecan pie. Buck appeared again, this time with presents.

"I think Santa left these in our car for any boys who might be around."

"That's me!" Zane jumped up and grabbed the gift, tearing into the red wrapping.

"What do you say?" Matt placed a hand on his son's head.

"Thank you," was the resounding answer from both boys.

Lank's sister suddenly appeared in front of the fireplace holding a Gibson guitar. "Found this in Mom's back closet, Lank. I think it belonged to our grandfather Torres. I know she would want you to have it. And you have to play something for us."

Lank's face turned white and then blushed pink as he stood up. Carli remembered the first night she arrived at the Wild Cow, she had heard music coming from the saddle house.

He cleared his throat and walked closer. As he took the guitar from his sister's hands, he studied it carefully.

"Sing, Uncle Lank."

"Please."

Anxious pleas from his nephews broke the silence. The boys set aside their new trucks and turned their attention to their uncle.

Lank strummed the guitar for a few minutes. "Carli, this one's for you." Lank shot her that sideways, mischievous grin that made her heart skip a beat and then began to sing.

> *Over the river and through the woods*
> *To Grandmother's house we go.*
> *The horse knows the way to carry the sleigh*
> *Through white and drifted snow.*
> *Over the river and through the woods,*
> *Oh, how the wind does blow.*
> *It stings the toes and bites the nose*
> *As over the ground we go.*

Lank ended with a flourishing strum on the guitar. His nephews clapped and giggled and turned big grins to Carli.

"Ha ha, very funny. Thanks for reminding me about how cold I was." Despite the frown she gave him, Carli couldn't hold in her laughter for very long.

As the merriment quieted, Lank cleared his throat and strummed a few notes. "This next one is for my mother, our mother. It was her favorite." He smiled at his sister and then closed his eyes for a minute. Carli held her breath, hoping he could make it through the song. He strummed a few more notes and then his clear, deep voice echoed through the living room rising above the crackling of the burning logs in the fireplace.

> *O Holy Night!*
> *The stars are brightly shining*
> *It is the night of the dear Savior's birth!*
> *Long lay the world in sin and error pining*
> *Till he appear'd and the soul felt its worth.*
> *A thrill of hope the weary soul rejoices*
> *For yonder breaks a new and glorious morn!*

The others remained silent, as if holding their breath. Lank stopped singing. He lowered his head and swiped the back of his hand across one cheek.

Lola stepped next to him and laid her hand on his shoulder. She began the chorus, "Fall on your knees."

The others joined in. Carli could barely sing through the tears that had formed in her eyes as she watched Lank strum his guitar while they sang. She saw the muscle of his jawline flex. He opened his mouth several times but shut it again without a sound. He closed his eyes and strummed his guitar while they all sang.

To break the solemn mood that fell over the group, Carli suggested her favorite. "How about 'We Wish you a Merry Christmas'?" With that they sang along and ended with smiles all around.

"It's late. We need to go." Kelly gathered coats and hats and ushered her bunch towards the front door. "Can we stay with Uncle Lank?" one nephew pleaded but the answer was a shake of his mother's head.

"Uncle Lank is very tired, boys." His sister turned towards Carli. "Sorry to run out so early, but I need to get these little guys in bed. Santa Claus arrives early at our house on Christmas morning. I'm so glad you're okay and it's really good to finally meet you." She gave Carli a hug.

Carli was taken aback by her sincere words and the warm hug. She didn't know what to say in reply, so she stood there like a mannequin. Finally, she muttered a weak, "Thank you."

"Yes, we are so glad to have Carli back safe and sound," said Lola, coming to Carli's rescue.

Lank hung back in front of the fireplace, studying the guitar he held in his hands. He finally placed the instrument on a dining room chair and hurried outside behind his sister and her family.

"Let's get these dishes done so you can go to bed, young lady. I know you must be exhausted. Even if you did have that big nap." Lola hurried to the kitchen. Lank came back in, and, with his and Buck's help, they had the kitchen cleared in no time. Carli refused some of the leftovers, insisting that Lola take some as well. She wished she had thought to send some home with Kelly.

Carli had never enjoyed a Christmas Eve more, but she was bone tired. Her eyelids were heavy, and it was all she could do to not collapse on the sofa.

"Good night, dear," said Lola. "We'll see you tomorrow. And Merry Christmas!"

"Thanks, Lola. Buck. Rena, too. Thanks for everything." She walked them to the door, waved goodbye, and then turned to see Lank still standing by the fireplace watching her. A bit mischievous, like he was about to grin but also with longing. The look in his eyes scared her. What was he planning?

"I'm sorry about your mother. That was a beautiful song and tribute to her. You're an amazing singer." She walked into the room, closing the gap between them. She wanted to melt into his arms, but her steps slowed. "Thanks again, Lank. I probably wouldn't have made it through this weekend without you. I owe you big time, but would you settle for a holiday hug from a boss to her employee?" Carli laughed, pushing the thought of that kiss in the barn from her mind.

She needed to keep this on a professional level. She leaned closer and raised up on her tiptoes but as she moved in for the hug, he turned his cheek away and instead planted a kiss on her lips. It wasn't a quick one either. His lips were warm and a tad sweet from the coffee and pie, and he pulled her close into a circle of warmth and safety as his arms came up around her. She couldn't stop the sigh that escaped her lips, but then came to her senses.

She drew back with a start. "What was that?"

"Mistletoe." He pointed over his right shoulder to a cluster of plastic greenery hanging near the top of the tree.

"Technically, we're not under it and I'm not sure that's what it is. I might have to fire you for sexual harassment." A little grin escaped her face.

"Being in the unemployment line will be worth it." And with that he grabbed his guitar, jammed his cowboy hat on his head, and left. The bang of the front door echoed through the now empty house.

Carli closed her eyes and willed her heart to slow down. "Best present ever," she whispered.

Chapter Thirty-Eight

Sunday, Christmas Morning, Wild Cow Ranch Head-quarters

Carli woke with a start and forced herself to push the covers back. She had slept late, still trying to recover from her night in the neighbor's barn. Nathan would be arriving any minute to pick her up and take her to the Olsen family Christmas Day festivities. She sank back on her bed, dreading the hustle of people and the smile she'd have to plant on her face for the remainder of the day. Sometimes she felt so fake. At some point these people would see who she really was. How can they all be so neighborly? It was exhausting at times.

She had to smile as memories of last night, her first time hosting a Christmas Eve dinner, came to mind. It had been a lot of fun. She hoped her Grandmother Jean and Grandpa Ward were looking down, knowing that Carli had found her way back to the Wild Cow Ranch at last. And that kiss flittered through her mind too. She pushed the memory away with a humpff.

Carli dressed quickly. Digging in her grandmother's closet she found a red sweater with a white, sparkling snowflake across the front. She and Lank had stacked the empty boxes from the basement against the wall. It would take her weeks to take down decorations and put everything back in its place. Inside one of the boxes, she found photo albums. Carli kneeled on the floor to take a look. In colors of gold, green, and red, the cover crackled when opened. Inside were plastic sleeves full of pictures from Christmases past. She recognized her grandmother and grandfather, but many of the other faces she didn't know. She smiled at the images of a much younger Buck and Lola, their arms linked and always together in every photo. A beautiful little girl commanded the center of attention in many of the photos. Her mother, Michelle. And then the photos stopped about halfway through. The back of the album was empty.

When Michelle turned into a rebellious teenager and left, Carli could have filled that void. She wished she had been given the chance. Stop it. There she was dwelling on the past again.

All those people and events she'd never be a part of. Why did she keep dredging up years that were gone, evaporated? She wanted to go back in time, change things. She wanted to demand that her guardians, the Fitzgeralds, take her to see her grandparents. Why hadn't she done that? A tear trickled down her cheek. The past was gone. Her wishing something would never make it so.

She squared her shoulders. Time to start making

new memories. She padded to the entry hall closet in her socks to find a coat and muffler. Tugging on her Grandmother Jean's turquoise boots which sat on the rug by the front door, her hand paused on the doorknob. She turned and walked to the Christmas tree. Carefully lifting the horse ornament and then removing the hanger, she admired the sparkles twinkling from the light streaming through the window.

"I'm here now, Grandma. I know you loved this time of year. God will lead me to my purpose. I'll try to make you proud." She placed the horse in her coat pocket.

Every decoration that had been stored in the basement was unpacked and out. She promised everyone the holiday shindig hosted by the Wild Cow would be a reality again next year, and here she was wearing a red sweater for a neighbor's Christmas dinner. Let the merrymaking begin, which was against her better judgment. Dang. No one took a picture of their dinner last night. She would make sure they did next time so that she could add her own pictures to the photo album. She hurried to the front door, grabbed a coat, and went outside to wait for Nathan.

After Nathan pulled into the driveway with a big grin and a wave, she took out her cell phone, opened the door, and snapped a pic. He sure was handsome wearing a bright red, pearl snap shirt for the occasion and a black cowboy hat.

"What'd you do that for?"

"Just making memories."

"Are you ready for the wildest Olsen celebration you've ever seen in your life? My brother and sisters are rowdy, you know." Nathan chuckled.

"Bring it on." Carli laughed. "And you can turn the radio to that jolly holly cheery channel, or whatever it's called."

"Seriously? Who are you and what have you done with my neighbor?" They laughed. "First, I have this for you." Nathan handed her a bright red box tied with green ribbon and a bow that was as big as the box.

Carli's heart dropped. She hadn't thought about buying a present for him, or anybody for that matter. She never had to worry about it before. She might as well come clean.

"Thanks, but I didn't get you anything. It's been a crazy week." She hesitated to take the gift, but he shoved it towards her, finally dropping it in her lap. She had no choice but to accept.

Slowly she tugged on the green ribbon.

"I'd like to eat sometime today, if you don't mind hurrying it up." Nathan turned sideways in the seat to look at her.

"I guess we're not leaving until I open this?"

"That's right."

She slid the ribbon off and opened the lid to see a wad of striped red and green tissue paper. "Perfect. What I've always wanted."

Nathan laughed. "Clever."

The tissue paper was wound tight and there was a lot of it. As she struggled, she glanced up at Nathan as he watched her intently, a wide boyish grin covering his handsome face. Inside was a clump of nuts and bolts and small copper rods. She turned it over and over in her hand, confused but with a planted smile on her face.

"It's Maverick." He grinned.

"Oh," was all Carli could manage. And then as she studied it, the shape of a cow began to emerge. The rods were his legs, his body was a huge bolt, two nuts welded together formed a head, and he had two tiny horns and floppy ears. The whole thing stood about four inches tall.

"A cow!" she exclaimed with delight. "You welded me a little cow. You made this?"

"Found a few things lying around the shop, plus I had to include nuts in honor of Maverick being able to keep his." They both laughed.

"I love it. It's perfect. Thank you, Nathan." She couldn't hold back the tears that clouded her eyes, and she couldn't look away from his gift. Although it was miniature in size, it was heavy. "I'm putting it on my desk."

"I'm glad you like it." Nathan shifted the pickup truck and turned out of her driveway.

"You do have a talent for this kind of thing, ya know."

"It's just a hobby." Nathan rolled through headquarters and slowed to bump across the cattle guard. "Are you ready for the famous Olsen family Christmas extravaganza?"

"I have a question. Would your mother by any chance know how to make snowmen out of toilet paper rolls?"

"Oh no. Don't tell me you're crafty too. We had to make a special ornament every year. It was a huge undertaking because Mom wanted us to make enough for everyone we know, and the list kept growing. I'm able to slip out to the barn these days but be warned. If you ask her, you may be stuck in the craft room until New Year's."

Carli laughed and glanced over at the corral. Lank stood alone, watching them, his arms resting on top of the pipe rail fence. The perfect image of a Texas cowboy, hat, purple wild rag, jean jacket, with one boot resting on the bottom rail of the fence. Good. He had fed the horses. She didn't wave and neither did he. She shouldn't have to wave every time an employee came into view. She was the boss. But it seemed rude that neither of them acknowledged the other.

As they drove away her lips tingled. That kiss, more than one to be exact, was something else. Even though she had spent many Christmases alone, her heart tugged at the sight of Lank standing by himself. She could still hear his clear, deep voice, see every detail of his handsome face as he sang last night. The musical notes from his guitar swirled in her head. That's the image of Christmas she would hold in her heart. The one that would be burned into her memory forever.

Her first Wild Cow Ranch Christmas.

Check out, Follow a Wild Heart (Wild Cow Ranch 3)

Finally settling into life on a Texas cattle ranch, Carli Jameson feels as if there is still something missing from her everyday routine. She realizes she misses her horse training clients and the successful business she left behind in Georgia – that's when the idea strikes her, she's going to open a riding school at Wild Cow Ranch.

After an uphill battle, opening day of LoveJoy Riding School is an utter disaster and Carli wants to give up. Turning to God for answers she decides to keep pushing forward, she now has troubled teenagers for students and needs to put their needs ahead of her own.

Managing her new-found obligations would be easier if she didn't have to confront the Texas cowboys that keep crossing her path – there's no time for romance when there's a ranch to run...or is there?

AVAILABLE NOW

About Natalie Bright

With roots firmly planted in the Texas Panhandle, Natalie Bright grew up obsessed with the Wild West and making up stories. The small farming community where she lived gave her a belief in hard-working, genuine people and a firm foundation of faith. She is the author of books for kids and adults, as well as numerous articles.

This author and blogger writes about small town heroes with complicated pasts and can-do attitudes, who navigate life's crazy misfortunes with humor and happy endings. A passionate supporter of history and libraries, Natalie loves exploring museums and collecting old books. Her ranch photography is featured in a chuck wagon cookbook. She lives on a dirt road with her husband, where they raise black and red Angus cattle and where the endless Texas sky continues to be her inspiration.

About Denise F. McAllister

Lovers of the West can be born in the most un-likely of places. For Denise F. McAllister, her start was in Miami, Florida, surrounded by beaches and the Everglades.

After being in the working world for some years, Denise F. McAllister decided to apply her life experience and study for her B.A. in communications and M.A. in professional writing. She loved going back to college "later in life" and hardly ever skipped a class as in her younger years. Growing up in the suburbs of Miami, Denise credits her love of horseback riding and showing in Atlanta, Georgia (15 years) for her heartfelt connection to all things Western.

Denise's faith is important to her and she loves to write about characters' journeys as they navigate real-world challenges. She prays that readers will enjoy her books, but most importantly experience a blessed connection with their Creator and Heavenly Father.

www.ingramcontent.com/pod-product-compliance
Lightning Source LLC
Chambersburg PA
CBHW011454170626
46814CB00009B/3048